SMOKE ON THE WIND

by Janet Shaw

✪ American Girl®

A Peek into
KAYA'S
WORLD

When snow began to fall in the high country, most Nez Perce families returned to their permanent villages in the protected canyons. There, they cooked and slept in long, mat-covered houses. Each longhouse was home to several families—and sometimes the entire village!

KAYA'S FAMILY and FRIENDS

Toe-ta
Kaya's father,
an expert horseman and
wise village leader

Wing Feather and Sparrow
Kaya's mischievous twin brothers

Eetsa
Kaya's mother, who is
a good provider for her
family and her village

Brown Deer
Kaya's older sister, who will
soon be old enough to marry

Pi-lah-ka and Kautsa
Eetsa's parents, who guide
and comfort Kaya

Speaking Rain
A blind girl who lives with
Kaya's family and is a sister to Ka

Tatlo
Kaya's sweet pup

Steps High
Kaya's beloved horse

White Braids
A kind woman who saves
Speaking Rain's life

Swan Circling
A strong warrior woman
whom Kaya admires

Two Hawks
A Salish boy who is a
friend to Kaya

Raven
A boy who loves to race horses

Fox Tail
A bothersome boy
who can be rude

KAYA
of the Nimíipuu People

Kaya and her family are Nimíipuu, known today as Nez Perce Indians. They speak the Nez Perce language, so you'll see some Nez Perce words in this book. "Kaya" is short for the Nez Perce name Kaya'aton'my', which means "she who arranges rocks." You'll find the meanings and pronunciations of these and other Nez Perce words in the glossary on page 106.

TABLE of CONTENTS

RUNAWAY HORSE!

❀ Chapter 1 ❀

Kaya knelt on a mat in the winter lodge and leaned over the baby named Light On The Water, who lay in her *tee-kas*. "*Tawts may-we!*" Kaya crooned to her. "Are you unhappy this morning?"

tee-kas

Light On The Water gazed steadily into Kaya's eyes, but her mouth trembled and turned down as if she was about to cry.

Kaya stroked the baby's plump, warm cheek. "Are you wet? Is that what you're telling me?" she asked. She loosened the lacing of the buckskin that wrapped the baby and pulled it away from her feet and legs. The soft cattail fluff that cushioned the baby's bottom was soaked. Kaya pulled it out, dried the baby, and placed fresh fluff underneath her. She squeezed one of the baby's little toes and kissed her forehead. Light On The Water smiled now. "*Tawts!*" Kaya said as she laced up the covering again.

Running Alone, Kaya's young aunt, put her hand on Kaya's shoulder. "Won't you make the lacing just a little tighter?" she asked. "We're going to ride out to gather wood for the fires, and I want my baby very safe."

Kaya tightened the lacing, then carried the baby out of the lodge. The day was chilly, and Light On The Water's breath was a small cloud at her lips. When Running Alone had mounted her horse, Kaya handed her the baby. Running Alone slipped the carrying strap of the tee-kas over her saddle horn and gazed down at her smiling daughter. "She likes your gentle touch," she told Kaya.

"She's so easy to care for," Kaya said. "Not like my little brothers. Look, they think I can't see them hiding behind that tree." She pointed at the two sets of dark eyes gleaming through the branches of a pine. "Boys, let's go riding!" she called to the twins, Wing Feather and Sparrow, and they came running, clutching robes of spotted fawn skin around their shoulders. Like all *Nimíipuu* children, they loved to be on horseback.

Kaya helped one twin climb up behind her older sister, Brown Deer. Then Kaya mounted a chestnut mare and lifted up the other twin. As she waited for the other women and children to mount, she glanced up toward the north. The foothills of the distant mountains were already white-robed with snow, but here in Salmon River Country the earth was still brown and bare. Each winter, Kaya's band came to these sheltering hills to make their winter

village. They put up their lodges near the banks of the
stream and stayed until spring, when it was time to move
up to the prairie to dig nourishing roots and bulbs for food.

Kaya pulled her elk robe more tightly around her
shoulders. Even dressed warmly in fur-lined moccasins,
leggings, and her robe, Kaya shivered in the chill of winter. But she remembered the heat of late summer, when
enemies from Buffalo Country made a raid on her people
to steal horses. Kaya's horse, Steps High, was stolen with
other Nimíipuu horses. And in the raid Kaya and her
sister Speaking Rain were captured as slaves and taken
far away to the enemy camp. There they met a *Salish* boy,
Two Hawks, who was also held as a slave. Kaya and Two
Hawks had managed to escape and cross the mountains
back to her people. But Speaking Rain, who was blind, had
insisted that she couldn't keep up—that Kaya must leave
her behind.

Kaya shivered again. She remembered, too, how cold—
and hungry!—she and Two Hawks had been as they made
their way over the Buffalo Trail. Now she and the boy were
safe, fed by the meat and warmed by the hides of animals
that had given themselves to her people. But Two Hawks
had broken his ankle on the trail, and it was slow to heal.

Kaya felt as if she had two aches in her chest. One ache
was a sharp-edged gratitude that she was with her family

again. But the other was a stab of grief that Speaking Rain was still a captive. Kaya had promised that they would be together again, but where was her sister now? If Kaya could find her, how could she save her? And would she ever see her beautiful, beloved horse again?

Soon Kaya was riding single file with the others. After a time, they came to a bowl-shaped canyon where trees grew thickly. The children ran to play, and the women fanned out along the creek to gather wood. A girl named Little Fawn and some boys were climbing aspen saplings and swinging to and fro on them.

"Magpie, fly into the trees with us!" Little Fawn called to Kaya.

Magpie! Kaya winced. She tried to ignore that awful nickname the children had given her when they were all punished because she hadn't taken care of her little brothers.

"Not now!" she called back. "I'm going to look for more fluff for the baby."

She glanced toward Light On The Water and Running Alone, who was tethering her horse to a tree. The baby, lulled by the rocking ride, napped in her tee-kas on the saddle horn. Taking a twined bag, Kaya started for the stream after the other women.

Suddenly, a sharp crack echoed across the canyon. Kaya

whirled around—the branch Little Fawn was pulling on had broken off. Little Fawn jumped to the ground. The branch slashed down like a spear and struck the rump of Running Alone's horse. The startled horse reared up in alarm and broke her tether. Wild-eyed, the panicked horse began to bolt down the canyon, the baby in the tee-kas still hanging in the saddle!

"Stop! Stop!" Running Alone cried out. She ran after the galloping horse.

Kaya ran, too. The fleeing horse was already halfway down the canyon and heading for the narrow opening and open country beyond. The tee-kas bumped against the horse's shoulder with each plunging step. Would the baby be tossed off? Light On The Water could be hurt badly—or killed!

Near the canyon opening, the young woman named Swan Circling came rushing from the woods. Dropping her robe behind her, she ran swiftly to cut off the horse's escape. She reached the opening of the canyon first and spun around to face the galloping horse, which was thundering straight at her. Taking a stand, she spread her arms wide, like an eagle in flight.

Would the horse run her down? Swan Circling stood her ground. Right in front of her, the runaway skidded to a halt. The horse snorted and tossed its head, flinging lather onto both Swan Circling and the baby.

Swan Circling seized the horse's reins. She held the horse firmly in place as Running Alone came rushing to get her baby.

Running Alone lifted the tee-kas from the saddle horn and clutched it to her chest. "My little one!" she cried, kissing her baby's face over and over. "You saved my baby, Swan Circling! *Katsee-yow-yow!* I can never thank you enough!"

Kaya came running right behind her aunt. She reached up to take hold of the reins, too, and stroked the horse's neck and shoulder to calm her.

"I saw you step in front of my horse, but how did you get her to halt?" Running Alone asked. "She could have run right past you—or right over you!"

"I didn't think of that," Swan Circling said. "I wanted her to stop, and she did. Is your baby all right?"

Light On The Water was grinning. She thought the bouncing, runaway ride was a game.

Swan Circling glanced at Kaya, who was still stroking the horse's lathered neck. "You seem to have a way with horses," she said approvingly. "She's quieting down. Will you lead her back now?"

Kaya held the reins of the uneasy horse securely as she and Swan Circling returned to the others. As they walked, she studied Swan Circling's calm face. Kaya had been curious about Swan Circling ever since she had married Claw Necklace and joined the band. And now Kaya remembered that the woman who appeared to her when she was lost on the Buffalo Trail had looked like Swan Circling. Had that vision been a sign that they would be friends? Kaya hoped so. She wished she could become as strong as this brave young woman who hadn't even flinched when a horse charged straight at her!

FEARLESS

Chapter 2

LATER THAT DAY, KAYA SAT WITH
other girls and women at one end of a lodge that several
families shared. Many layers of tule reed mats and hides
covered the lodge. Piles of hide blankets and painted
parfleches filled with extra clothing and
supplies were stacked along the bottom to
keep out drafts. The women unfolded the
hides they'd tanned in the summer and set
about making moccasins and clothes and
carrying cases. They took out the hemp
cord they'd twisted and wove baskets and
bags. They made their clothes beautiful with

parfleche

fringe and beads and quill decorations. Kaya loved working with the others in the warm winter lodge.

Kaya's mother, *Eetsa*, was finishing a large twined storage bag, one of the many gifts they would give to family
and friends when they came to visit.

Kautsa, Kaya's grandmother, was weaving a small
hat. Kaya watched her grandmother's expert work

closely—because the hat was for her. Kaya would wear it in the spring when she went to dig roots with the other girls and women.

Kaya put aside the basket she was weaving and picked up her sister's worn buckskin doll. Speaking Rain had carried her doll everywhere she went. With her sister gone, Kaya kept the doll close to her. As she adjusted the doll's dress, she discovered a tear in her back, a bit of deer-hair stuffing poking out. She decided to mend it and have it ready for Speaking Rain when she was with them again.

Kaya wanted to care for the doll because she feared she hadn't taken good care of Speaking Rain. When the enemies had made their raid in the night last summer, Eetsa had told Kaya to take Speaking Rain to hide in the woods. But Kaya went first to look for her horse—and enemies seized her and her sister and carried them off. How Kaya regretted that she hadn't done as her mother told her! *If I were as strong as Swan Circling,* Kaya thought, *I'd find a way to get my sister back.*

"Kautsa, may I ask you a question?" Kaya asked quietly.

"*Aa-heh,* you may ask me anything," Kautsa said. A slight smile crinkled the corners of her eyes. "Ask—then I'll decide if I want to answer you."

"You're teasing," Brown Deer said, laughing. "You always answer us!"

"It's true," Kautsa said. "I've always answered your questions—so far! What do you want to know?"

Kaya threaded her bone needle with a bit of sinew and began stitching the tear in the buckskin doll. "I want to ask about Swan Circling. What makes her so . . . different?"

"Different?" Kautsa said. "You must be asking me how Swan Circling came to be a warrior woman. Now, there's a story!"

"Can you tell us?" Brown Deer said eagerly.

Kautsa nodded. Her fingers were busy as she twined brown hemp with yellow bear grass. "Swan Circling came to live with us when she and Claw Necklace married, three winters ago. We all saw right away that she was a strong girl, eager to help. Then . . ." Kautsa paused and held the hat she was weaving above Kaya's head to check the size. The many strands of cord trailing from the hat tickled Kaya's nose.

"Then?" Kaya prompted her grandmother.

"Then?" Brown Deer echoed. "What happened then, Kautsa?"

Kautsa put the hat back into her lap and began to work on it again. "Then Swan Circling went with her husband on a hunting trip to Buffalo Country. While they slept one night, enemies attacked them!"

"To steal horses, as they did with us?" Kaya asked.

"Not to steal horses," Kautsa said. "They came to fight—or to show their courage just by touching our warriors! Our men rushed from the tepees to defend themselves. Claw Necklace hurried into the skirmish. But in his eagerness to fight, he left behind his bow and arrows."

"He didn't have any weapons?" Kaya asked.

"Aa-heh, he was in great danger!" Kautsa said. "Instead of running for cover with the other women, Swan Circling picked up his weapons and ran after him into the fight. Arrows flew around her. One even singed her arm, but it didn't pierce her flesh. She gave her husband the bow and arrows so he could fight well, and then she tended our wounded men. She was never wounded by arrows, though a few tore her dress."

"Did Swan Circling tell you this?" Kaya asked.

"She would never speak of her bravery," Kautsa said. "It was Claw Necklace who told us what had happened. After our men won the fight, they gave Swan Circling an eagle feather for her bravery—a very high honor, as you know."

"I know she goes to battles," Brown Deer said. "She brings fresh horses to the riders whose horses have been hurt."

"So she does," Kautsa said. "Swan Circling has brought many things to us. You were with her when she saved

Running Alone's baby, weren't you, Kaya?"

"Aa-heh, Kautsa," Kaya said. "I saw it all."

"Then you know she's fearless," Kautsa said. "I believe she wouldn't hesitate to fight a grizzly bear! There's only one sad thing—"

Brown Deer stopped stringing beads and looked up. "What sad thing?" Brown Deer asked.

"As you know, Swan Circling doesn't have any children. That's sad, don't you think?" Kautsa asked.

"It would be very sad not to have any children," Brown Deer said slowly, as if she were imagining how she'd feel if she were Swan Circling.

"But she and her husband are young," Eetsa broke in. "There's still plenty of time for them to have children."

"Aa-heh," Kautsa agreed. "There's time for children. And they'll be strong, like her, I'm sure of that." Then she tapped Kaya's hand. "I'm glad you mended your sister's doll, Granddaughter."

Eetsa rose to her knees and peered into the cooking basket. "We need some water so we can cook our meal," she announced.

Right away Kaya got to her feet to go fetch the water. She caught up with Little Fawn on the trail to the stream. Like Kaya, Little Fawn carried a large water basket, but she was limping. "Did you hurt yourself when the branch broke?" Kaya asked. "Maybe you climbed too high."

Little Fawn winced at each step, but she shook her head. "It's nothing. I've jumped out of trees much higher than that."

Other women and girls were drawing water at the stream. Kaya saw Swan Circling a little way downstream, leading a spotted mare. As the mare drank, Swan Circling dampened a bundle of leaves and tied it onto the mare's back. Kaya went downstream to her side. She'd been eager to see Swan Circling again, but now that she stood beside her, she didn't know what to say. She stroked the mare's flank. "This is a pretty one," Kaya said. "Has she got sores on her back?"

"Aa-heh," Swan Circling said. "The men saw her rolling in a patch of sage to heal herself. They asked me to make a poultice of the sage for her."

"The spots on her rump remind me of my horse, Steps—" Kaya stopped, afraid to go on for fear her voice would break.

Swan Circling glanced at her with concern in her eyes. "You miss your horse, don't you?" she said. "I just saw the boy who escaped with you."

Kaya leaned out and dipped her water basket into the stream. "Two Hawks can't put weight on his broken ankle yet," she said.

"It takes time for bone to heal," Swan Circling said.

"He doesn't like to be patient!" Kaya said.

Swan Circling laughed. "That's the kind of boy he is!
It's good you were with him when you escaped. You're a
dependable girl, I can see that. You two were very strong to
run away and find your way back."

Kaya's cheeks burned with pleasure at this praise from
the woman she admired so much. To keep Swan Circling
from seeing that she was blushing, Kaya turned her head.

Little Fawn was standing on the shore a little way
upstream with a basket of water in her arms. When Kaya
looked her way, Little Fawn lifted her chin and narrowed
her eyes. "Magpie flew back to her nest!" she said, and
limped away. Was she jealous of the praise Kaya had been
given?

"Magpie?" Swan Circling said. "Is that your nickname,
Kaya?" She patted the mare's rump and took her lead rope.

"They call me that sometimes," Kaya said.

Swan Circling gave Kaya a searching look. "Some
nicknames dig into us like bear claws," she said. "As you
grow older, they don't hurt so much. Will you remember
that, Kaya?"

"Aa-heh," Kaya said. "I'll remember."

"Tawts," Swan Circling said with approval. She started
to lead the mare back to the men who tended the horses.

Kaya bit her lip as she watched Swan Circling walking back to the herd. Swan Circling had offered her good advice about her nickname. But, of course, she didn't know that Kaya had gotten it last summer because she'd gone off to race her horse instead of taking care of her younger brothers. Whipwoman had scolded Kaya, saying she must learn to think of others before she thought of herself. If Swan Circling knew that, she'd certainly regret calling Kaya strong—or dependable. And if she knew it was Kaya's fault that she and Speaking Rain had been taken captive, she doubted Swan Circling would have any respect for her at all.

LESSONS FROM A BASKET

Chapter 3

OVERNIGHT IT HAD GROWN COLDER.
A sharp wind whined around the lodge where Kaya and
other children were dressing after their morning swim. But
the lodge was warmed by five fires in a line down the
center, smoke rising through the long opening at the top.
Eetsa and the other women were already cooking a morning meal because there was much work to do that day.

Kaya knew that soon friends and family would come
from other villages nearby for the new year celebration,
when the short winter days begin to grow longer again.
People would share their news and give each other gifts.
They'd feast and tell stories and honor *Hun-ya-wat,* who
made the seasons and held them in balance.

Today the women were putting up another lodge, one
large enough to hold everyone for the feasts. When Kaya
joined them, she saw Swan Circling helping to raise one of
the long lodge poles and set it onto the frame of tepee poles.
Kaya thought the framework looked like the backbone and
ribs of a skeleton of a huge horse. After the women

completed the frame, they would cover it with tule mats and hides. Kaya helped other girls carry the rolled-up mats and place them near the builders. She kept Swan Circling in sight, hoping to have a chance to talk with her again.

When the lodge was finished, Kaya followed Swan Circling to another lodge, where women were preparing more food so that there would be enough for the visitors. Eetsa and Running Alone were making pemmican, a mixture of dried meat and berries. With a stone pestle, they were pounding dried deer meat in a large mortar. When one of them got tired using the heavy stone pestle, they traded places. Kaya thought the steady *thump, thump, thump* sounded like a heartbeat.

Swan Circling joined the women, and Kaya went to peek at Light On The Water, who was snug in her tee-kas.

"Would you give my baby a piece of this dried meat?" Running Alone asked Kaya. "She's getting a new tooth, and she needs something to chew on." She turned back to breaking strips of the meat and putting the pieces into the mortar to be ground fine.

Kaya broke off a bit of the meat and held it to Light On The Water's lips. But the baby pressed her lips shut tightly, her eyes merry as if she and Kaya were playing a game.

"Isn't she precious!" Kaya exclaimed. Then she glanced at
Swan Circling. Kautsa had said it was sad that she had no
children yet. Did she mind that Kaya was a making a fuss
over the baby?

Swan Circling was using the large pestle. Her strong
arms gleamed with sweat from the hard work. "When I
saw you girls in the stream this morning, I thought of the
time when I was your age," she said when Kaya caught her
eye. "Do you like to swim?"

"Aa-heh!" Kaya said.

"So do I," Swan Circling said. "I come from a place
where the Snake River joins the Big River. My friends and
I swam every chance we got. My mother called us the Fish
Girls. Someday I'll show you my favorite places to dive
from the cliffs, Kaya."

"You're always thinking of the future, aren't you?"
Eetsa said to Swan Circling. "Many times I've heard you
say 'someday this' or 'someday that.'"

"It's true," Swan Circling said. She smiled at Eetsa, who
was her good friend, and passed her the pestle. Then she
wiped her face with the back of her hand. "Do you often
think of what's to come, Kaya?"

Kaya was thinking that no one ever asked her as many
questions about herself as Swan Circling did. Kaya liked
that. "I think of seeing my horse again," Kaya said. "Mostly

I think of getting my little sister back. But I don't know how I can do that."

"When a way opens, you'll be ready," Swan Circling said with confidence.

Kaya gently rocked the baby in the tee-kas. Lulled by the motion and the voices of the women, Light On The Water was falling asleep. Oh, how Kaya wanted to be the girl Swan Circling believed her to be. And how she feared she wasn't!

The next morning as Kaya stepped out of the stream where the girls had taken their morning swim, she saw Swan Circling beckoning to her. The frigid air made Kaya feel like running and jumping with energy. She pulled her elk robe around her and hurried to meet Swan Circling.

"Tawts may-we!" Kaya said.

"Aa-heh, tawts may-we, Kaya," Swan Circling said. "I have something I want to show you. Would you like to work with me today?"

"Aa-heh!" Kaya said. "If Kautsa says I may, I'll work with you."

"Run and ask her then," Swan Circling said. "I'll be in the lodge."

After Kautsa said that Kaya could work with Swan Circling, Kaya joined her again. Swan Circling was kneeling on a mat in the crowded lodge. Kaya knelt at her side and watched her untie the flaps of a large parfleche painted with triangle designs in red, blue, green, and yellow. "I saw you weaving with your grandmother. It reminded me of a basket I made when I was a little girl— my very first one."

"My first was awfully lopsided," Kaya said, "but I gave it to Kautsa anyway."

Swan Circling lifted out her special ceremonial dress and moccasins from the parfleche and set them aside. Then she took out a little brown twined basket and handed it to Kaya. "You can see that my first basket's lopsided, too."

Kaya smiled at the lumpy little basket. She liked to imagine Swan Circling as a girl with small hands and big ideas—a girl just like Kaya. "Didn't you give your first basket to your grandmother?" she asked.

Swan Circling nodded. "Aa-heh, I did. After she died, it was given back to me. I'm glad. This basket taught me many lessons."

Kaya turned it over. With her fingertip she traced the weaving. "Was one of the lessons to make your twining tighter?"

Swan Circling smiled. "Aa-heh, to pull the cord tighter was one thing I learned. But that wasn't all—I learned

about patience, too. I was a very bold, headstrong girl.
I thought that there was nothing I couldn't do!"

"But you can do everything, can't you?" Kaya asked.

Now Swan Circling laughed. "Of course I can't!" She
put her warm hand on Kaya's knee. "You see, I'd been
watching my grandmother weave her baskets, and I was
sure I knew how. I decided I was going to make a beautiful one just like hers. I got my basket started, but I made
mistake after mistake. Finally, I had this pitiful little thing
to show her."

"What did she say about it?" Kaya asked.

"She thanked me and said I'd made a start. But I
expected more praise than that," Swan Circling admitted.
"I remember I was pouting. I asked her why she hadn't
corrected my mistakes, as if the lumps in my basket were
her fault! Then she told me, 'Everyone has to have her own
lessons.' Little by little I understood that to make a mistake
is not a bad thing. But I should be wise enough not to make
the same mistake again—and again."

Kaya understood that Swan Circling wasn't speaking
now of basket making; she was speaking of life.

This was a chance for Kaya to tell Swan Circling about
how she'd gotten her nickname and why the enemies were
able to capture her and Speaking Rain—and about her
guilt for escaping without her sister. She could finally tell

Swan Circling the truth. "I've made mistakes, too," Kaya began. "I—"

Swan Circling waited for her to go on.

But Kaya lost her nerve. What if she told Swan Circling the truth, and her friend lost respect for her? If she did, she would no longer seek out Kaya. No, Kaya couldn't risk losing Swan Circling's friendship.

"I left holes in a basket I was making," Kaya said in a determined voice. "But my grandmother showed me right away so I could do a better job." She handed back the clumsy little basket.

Swan Circling repacked it with the other things and tied the parfleche. "Is something troubling you?" she asked Kaya. "There's a crease right here." She put a fingertip between Kaya's eyebrows.

Kaya didn't want to meet Swan Circling's gaze. "No, nothing's troubling me," she said.

Still Swan Circling waited. After a moment, she put the parfleche back on a stack against the lodge wall. "Maybe we've done enough talking," she said. "Come, let's pack up the pemmican and put it into storage."

THE LONGEST NIGHT

Chapter 4

K**AYA AND BROWN DEER WERE**
helping Kautsa take wrapped camas cakes from a storage
pit when a crier came riding through the village. "Friends
are arriving! Get ready for them!" he called out. Everyone
stopped what they were doing and gathered to welcome
their visitors.

A northeast wind, the coldest one, blew fine flakes of
snow. Kaya shaded her eyes as she watched the horizon.
Soon she saw a dark line of horses and riders come over
the snow-covered rise and descend on the village.

What could be better in this cold season than the
warmth of greeting friends and family! Everyone hugged
and smiled and talked and handed around gifts. Men,
women, and children crowded inside with their belongings
until all the lodges were pleasantly full.

Kaya's aunt from a nearby village greeted her with a
strong hug and a kiss. "Scouts told us about your capture
and escape," she said. "We're so glad you're well!"

"Did the scouts have news of my sister?" Kaya asked.

The smile left her aunt's face. "No one has any news of her," she said. "Of course, no one can cross the Buffalo Trail now. Our enemies must have taken her back to their country with them."

Biting her lip, Kaya turned away.

Swan Circling touched Kaya's arm. "Will you help me carry these baskets of food?" she asked Kaya gently. "We have so much to do for the gathering tonight."

When night came, Kaya and the others dressed in their best clothes and entered the ceremonial lodge for the new year gathering. This was the shortest day of the year—and the darkest. The clouds had cleared, and stars shone in the sky, where the new moon, thin as a fish bone, had risen. Four big tepees had been put together to make this lodge, but soon the large space was crowded with people.

Several men held a drum made of hide. The fires in the center of the lodge cast their light on the walls, and the air smelled sweetly of cedar boughs and tule mats.

When everyone was in the lodge, To Soar Like An Eagle raised his hand to get attention. He wore a feathered headdress and a painted hide shirt decorated with porcupine quills. He was a very respected old chief with white eyebrows and a low, powerful voice that came from deep in his chest. Kaya watched his lined face as he spoke.

"Hun-ya-wat has made this night longer than all the

others," To Soar Like An Eagle said. "In this darkest time, let us reflect on the days that have gone before and on the days that lie ahead. It is time to renew life."

The drummers began, filling the night with drumbeats that echoed back from the surrounding hills. After the drumming, men and women began to speak of births and deaths and of the gifts Hun-ya-wat had given them in the past year. They told of good deeds and acts of bravery. They gave thanks for successful hunts and for ample fish and roots and berries. Together they prayed that all might keep their minds and hearts pure so there would be enough food in the year to come.

Kaya listened closely to the prayer songs. She looked at her parents and grandparents standing near her. Firelight played over their solemn faces. Brown Deer, too, was sober and thoughtful. Even the twins, such lively little boys, seemed to be listening closely to the singing.

Two Hawks, the Salish boy she had run away with to escape enemy raiders, couldn't understand the words. He gazed steadily at the others as though he understood everything from their serious expressions.

Kaya could see Swan Circling standing with her young husband, Claw Necklace. Her dark eyes reflected the firelight, but her thoughts seemed far away, as if she was thinking of the future again.

Kaya considered her own life over the past year. She had much to be thankful for, but she had many regrets, too. Her good and bad feelings mingled like the streams of smoke rising from the fires. Her eyes smarted with them.

When Kaya glanced again at Swan Circling, she realized what was troubling her tonight—she hadn't yet told her friend how she got her nickname or how her disobedience had gotten her and Speaking Rain captured. She hadn't been brave enough. Until she shared that story, Swan Circling wouldn't really know her.

Kaya closed her eyes. *Hun-ya-wat, make me honest and strong in character,* she prayed silently. *Help me face life with an honorable, truthful, strong will.*

When the prayers came to an end, it was time for the midnight feast. Women brought out steaming salmon broth followed by bowls of mashed roots and berries. As Kaya watched the preparations, she felt a quiet, calm resolve in her heart. Her prayer had given her courage. She would tell Swan Circling everything—and as soon as possible.

A SICK BABY

✳ Chapter 5 ✳

KAYA WATCHED FOR A CHANCE TO
speak with Swan Circling, but with all the visitors crowded
into the lodges, they were never together. After several
days, the visitors left for their own villages. Now, surely,
Kaya could take Swan Circling aside and talk with her.

One morning Kaya was piling wood beside the cooking
fires when Running Alone hurried over.

"Would you look after my baby for a little while?"
Running Alone asked Kaya. "I'm troubled about her. I want
to find Bear Blanket and ask her for help."

Kaya was worried as she followed Running Alone
through the lodge to her sleeping place. Bear Blanket was
a powerful medicine woman who had cured many, many
sick people. Light On The Water must be sick, or Running
Alone wouldn't be looking for the medicine woman's help.

Light On The Water lay in a hide swing hung from the
lodge pines. Kaya leaned over her. The baby's face was
flushed, and each time she drew a breath she coughed.
Tiny beads of sweat covered her forehead and cheeks. Her

eyes were open, but she didn't gaze up at
Kaya. She didn't seem to see anything at all.

When Running Alone hurried off, Kaya
placed her finger in the baby's hot little
hand. Light On The Water didn't tug at it, as
she usually did. "Are you sick, little one?"
Kaya whispered. "There's help for you. You
won't be sick for long."

Soon Bear Blanket came through the door of the lodge.
She was an old, gray-haired woman, but her back was as
straight as an arrow. Kaya knew that Bear Blanket always
kept her mind and body clean so she would be ready to
help those who needed her. Her animal spirit helper was a
grizzly bear. Long ago she had received medicine power—
the power to heal—from this *wyakin*.

Bear Blanket carried a medicine bundle in one hand.
Swan Circling followed right behind her. Running Alone
motioned for Kaya to stand aside so that Bear Blanket
could see the baby. The old woman studied the baby's face
and bent over to listen to her coughing. Then she spread
her hands over the baby's head and began to sing one of
her medicine songs.

As she sang, she passed her hands up and down over
Light On The Water's body. Kaya saw the baby's eyelids
tremble and shut, then open again when she coughed

harder. Bear Blanket drew Swan Circling aside and spoke
to her and then went back to her singing.

Swan Circling frowned. "She wants me to bring her the
inner bark of a special tree to boil for a healing drink," she
said to Running Alone. "I'm going to get my horse and go
after it now."

"But it's very cold," Running Alone said. "The northeast
wind is blowing again. Will you be all right?"

"It can't wait," Swan Circling said. "Your baby needs
the medicine now."

Running Alone put her hand on Swan Circling's arm.
"Then hurry!" she urged her. "Kaya will round up your
horse for you while you get your blankets and your knife."

Kaya threw a deerskin over her shoulders and grabbed
a rope bridle. Her breath was a white plume at her lips as
she ran out to the herd grazing near the village. She found
Swan Circling's white-faced horse, placed the bridle on her
lower jaw, and rode her back to the lodges.

Swan Circling was wearing otter-skin leggings and
mittens and had her elk robe around her. She held her
beautiful saddle of wood and painted rawhide. Kaya
reined in the horse and slipped off. She put on the saddle
and reached under the horse's belly for the cinch. Already
Swan Circling was hanging her bags from the saddle horn.

"Cinch it snugly," Swan Circling told Kaya. "I'm going

to ride as fast as possible. Bear Blanket said the baby is very sick." She tested the saddle cinch with her weight and then swung up. "Good work, Kaya. I'll be back before last light. Watch for me." She urged her horse forward and, in a few strides, was running full out across the frozen ground.

"I'll watch for you!" Kaya called after her. But the wind snatched away her words.

All day Kaya stayed with Running Alone and her baby. Bear Blanket sang her medicine songs, but the baby only coughed harder and harder. Light On The Water's little face was red, and her eyes screwed shut with her effort to breathe. Kaya watched her anxiously—did the baby have the terrible sickness of blisters that the men with pale faces brought to the land? Kaya was afraid to ask.

As the light began to fade, Kaya went to watch for Swan Circling's return. At dusk there were no colors in the valley. The river was a shining black curve, like a snake, and the trees were black slashes against the white snow. Under dark clouds, a hawk rode the wind in slow, wide turns. *Where is Swan Circling?* Kaya thought. *Why doesn't she come back?*

Then she saw a horse appear in the trees at the far end of the valley. Kaya ran up the hillside a little way to get a better look. The horse had a white face—Swan Circling's horse. Kaya caught her breath in relief. But as the horse came closer, out of the trees, Kaya saw that it was limping as though it was hurt—and that it had no rider.

MEDICINE

✷ Chapter 6 ✷

KAYA WATCHED CLAW NECKLACE
and a small group of men saddle their horses and ride off
to search for Swan Circling. Kaya couldn't believe that anything bad could have happened—her friend was so young,
so strong. Maybe she'd fallen off her horse, and it had run
away from her. Surely she was coming home on foot and
the men would soon meet up with her. In the meantime,
here was her bag—still hanging on the saddle horn.

Kaya ran with the bag to find Bear Blanket. The
medicine woman was with Running Alone and her baby,
who lay gasping in the baby swing. Bear Blanket opened
the bag and took out a handful of bark. "This is the good
medicine I asked for," she said.

"Tawts!" Running Alone exclaimed. "I knew Swan
Circling wouldn't fail us."

Kaya dug her fingernails into her palms as she gazed
down at the baby's red face and dry lips. Would blisters
soon break out on her cheeks? Her people had never seen
the men with pale faces, but their sickness had killed many

Nimíipuu. "Tell me," she asked fearfully, "does the baby have the bad sickness that kills?"

"Not that," Bear Blanket said quickly. "She has a weakness in her chest."

Kaya unclenched her fists. "Will the medicine help?"

"I'll make a healing drink with it," Bear Blanket said. "Soon she'll breathe more easily. Go rest, Kaya. There's nothing you can do now."

Kaya was warm under a blanket of woven strips of rabbit fur, but she couldn't sleep. Her thoughts were with Swan Circling, who was somewhere in the darkness. Perhaps she'd built herself a lean-to for shelter, as Kaya had done when she escaped from the enemies. Or maybe, any moment now, Swan Circling would come walking into the lodge with Claw Necklace. She had to be all right!

Kaya slept fitfully. Before first light she awoke to a cold draft on her cheek. She pushed up onto her elbow. A few people were stirring in the lodge, and someone had pulled back the covering of the doorway. Had Swan Circling returned? Kaya crawled from underneath her blanket. She saw Eetsa leaving the lodge with a torch in her hand. Kaya pulled her elk robe around her shoulders, followed Eetsa to the door, and peeked out.

The moon had already set, and the sky was turning gray. In the space between the lodges, Eetsa joined a group of men and women. Kaya saw her grandparents, Kautsa and *Pi-lah-ka*, and other elders wrapped in their robes. Her father, *Toe-ta*, was talking with them. And now she made out Claw Necklace walking toward the lodges. He carried something. Kaya blinked. Then she realized it was Swan Circling that Claw Necklace held in his arms.

Kaya couldn't get her breath. No!—Swan Circling would be all right! She would be! Kaya pulled her robe over her head and hid her face in it.

In a moment she felt firm hands on her shoulders. She lifted her chin and looked up into Kautsa's face. In the gray early light, her grandmother looked very old and very tired. "Our men found her body beside the stream," Kautsa said quietly. "It seems her horse broke through thin ice and stumbled, and she was thrown off. Her head struck a boulder, and the blow killed her." She opened her arms and took Kaya into her warm embrace.

Through her tears, Kaya heard Kautsa's gentle voice at her ear. "She was full of light and love," Kautsa said. "It's hard to let her go, but we must help her spirit journey on."

Kaya walked in a daze after Swan Circling's death. She felt as if a jagged hole had been torn in her heart. Mixed in with the pain of her friend's death was another pain—one of regret. Oh, why hadn't she quickly called up the courage to tell Swan Circling everything? Now it was too late.

Everyone in the village grieved and mourned for Swan Circling. They comforted one another with gentle words and tried to console Claw Necklace, too. Runners took the bad news to neighboring villages. Though it was the heart of winter, one runner volunteered to travel all the way to the Big River to tell Swan Circling's family.

None of Swan Circling's family lived close enough to help with the burial, so the women in her husband's family took charge of the preparations. The best hide workers took out fresh white deer hides, clean and unused, to make a new dress and moccasins to clothe the body. Other women prepared food to serve the whole community after the burial ceremony. Some stayed with the body, never leaving it alone, even for a moment.

Kaya stayed close to Running Alone and her baby. The medicine had helped Light On The Water. She wasn't coughing so hard now, and she gazed up at Kaya's face when Kaya rocked the swing and sang to her. Light On The Water didn't need encouragement to sleep, though— she was still weak and listless.

Even when the baby slept, Kaya kept singing the lullaby, "She's the precious one, my own dear little precious one." She was sure Swan Circling was listening. Until her body was buried, her spirit would stay close by.

GIFTS FROM SWAN CIRCLING

Chapter 7

BEFORE FIRST LIGHT ON THE THIRD
morning after Swan Circling's death, Toe-ta and other men
went to the burial place on a rise above the stream to dig
a grave. When they sent word that the grave was ready,
everyone gathered in the faint light for the ceremony.

Swan Circling's body and some of her things had been
wrapped in clean hides and fresh mats and placed on a
horse-drawn travois. Fighting her tears, Kaya followed
with the others as the body was taken to the burial place—
which faced east, where the sky would soon brighten.

A medicine man with strong spirit powers led the way.
He was a short man with a broad chest and shoulders, and
he wore a fur headdress set with mountain sheep horns.
At the graveside, he praised Swan Circling's strength,
her unwavering courage, and her willingness to help her
people. He spoke of everyone's sorrow to lose such a good
woman. Then he urged her spirit to travel on.

As the first streak of dawn stained the pale sky, the
men placed the body in the shallow grave and covered

it with another mat. First the women and then the men
stepped one by one to the grave and dropped in a handful
of earth. When it was Kaya's turn, she vowed silently, *All
my life I'll think of you! I'll strive to be like you, I promise!*

But Swan Circling's spirit wouldn't be able to rest until
all her belongings had been given away or burned. Because
Eetsa had been a close friend of Swan Circling, she took
charge of the giveaway.

In the lodge, Eetsa placed all of Swan Circling's belongings on a mat. One by one, Toe-ta called friends and family
members to step forward. With a few words, he gave
Running Alone the mortar and pestle. Little Fawn received
the digging stick, and Kautsa a large parfleche. To Brown
Deer he gave a pair of deerskin moccasins. He gave other
women and girls Swan Circling's baskets, necklaces, shells,
and hides until there was nothing left on the mat by his
feet but Swan Circling's saddle.

Then Toe-ta motioned for Kaya to come forward. She
kept her gaze on her moccasins as her father spoke to her.
"Claw Necklace told me his wife admired your care for
horses and your love of them," he said gently. "He's certain
she would want you to have her saddle."

"Katsee-yow-yow," Kaya murmured.

Then Toe-ta rubbed his lips with his thumb. He thought
a moment. "She also wanted you to have something much

more important than a saddle," he said.

In his deep voice Toe-ta told how Swan Circling had recently come to him and Eetsa and asked to speak with them. "She told us she had a dark dream, a dream of her death," he said. "She wasn't frightened, but she said that if she should die, she wanted Kaya to have her name. As you know, her name was hers to give as she chose. She was fond of you, Kaya, and she spoke of your special friendship. She believed you would carry her name well. We accepted her gift to you with gratitude."

Now a very old woman lifted her head to speak. It was her job to remember how everyone was related to each other. "What Kaya's father says is true," she said firmly. "I was there when Kaya's parents accepted the name. I say this is so."

Kaya hugged the beautiful saddle of painted wood and hide that Toe-ta had handed her. But as she turned and walked back to her place, her mind couldn't take in the second gift that Swan Circling had given. Her name! That was the greatest gift anyone could give. Kaya's thoughts rushed back and forth between gratitude and doubt. How honored she was to have been given her friend's name! But could she truly be worthy of it? And would Swan Circling have given it if she'd known Kaya's failures? If only Swan Circling were here, for it seemed to Kaya that her friend

"She also wanted you to have something
much more important than a saddle," Toe-ta said.

was the one person who could quiet these racing doubts and fears. But Kaya was alone with her torn feelings.

It wasn't until that night that Kaya could talk with her mother. Eetsa had heated stones in the fire and was putting them into a water basket to boil deer meat. She stirred the hot stones rapidly to keep them from scorching the basket. Kaya crouched by her side.

"Eetsa, I'm troubled about my namesake," Kaya said, careful not to say the name of the dead out loud.

Eetsa lifted out the cooled stones with a forked stick and put in more hot ones. "What troubles you, Daughter?" she asked.

"I don't think she'd have given me her name if she'd known the mistakes I've made," Kaya admitted. "I never told her about my nickname or how it was my fault that Speaking Rain and I were taken captive."

When Eetsa glanced at her, Kaya saw her mother's eyes soften. "But there's nothing to be troubled about," Eetsa said. "She knew about your nickname, but she said it didn't matter to her. And she said it took great strength to leave your sister behind and that you were wise to do so."

"She said that to you?" Kaya asked.

"Aa-heh," Eetsa assured her. "She often spoke about you. She told me she had confidence that you would grow to be trustworthy and strong. And she said you have a

generous heart, Daughter—which you do. It's not time for
you to use her name yet, but when that time comes, you'll
know. Is there anything else troubling you?"

Kaya pressed her lips together and shook her head. Her
heart was full—she was afraid that if she spoke, she'd burst
into tears of both gratitude and relief.

The next morning, Kaya sat with her little brothers on
her rabbit-fur blanket. The twins lay on their stomachs
with their chins in their hands. They were watching as
she shaped and tied long pine needles to make three little
horses.

"Is one of those horses for me?" Wing Feather asked.

"If my brother gets a toy, so do I!" Sparrow demanded.
"Don't I, Kaya?"

"Yes, one of these horses is for you," she said, tapping
Wing Feather on his nose. "And one's for you," she told
Sparrow and tugged his braid.

Kaya put the finishing touches on the little horses and
handed one to each boy. "Here they are," she said. "Now
you can have races."

"Katsee-yow-yow!" the twins said at the same time.
They seized their toys and scampered with them to the pile
of hides where other children were playing.

Kaya cut a small piece of hide and tied it with a bit of

fringe onto the third little horse's back—there, now this one had a saddle. Then she wrapped herself in her elk robe and left the lodge without telling anyone where she was going. Since she'd wakened, she'd known what she must do.

The trail to the burial place led around some low hills. Bare trees cast blue shadows on the thin covering of snow. Coyotes hunting rabbits had left tracks in the snow, and Kaya saw the wing print of a hawk that had swooped down for a kill.

On the east-facing side of the hill, she turned off the trail. There were many graves here, marked with rocks. Mourners had left small gifts on some of them. Kaya went to the place Swan Circling was buried and put the little horse made of pine needles on her grave.

"I've been thinking about things," Kaya said softly to her friend. "I want you to know I'm going to live up to your expectations—and that I'm grateful for your trust. And your name. But I hope to get my sister back—and maybe my horse, too—before I use your name. I want to deserve what you've given me. I want our people to think well of me when they call me by your name."

Kaya looked back at her village. In the cold, only dogs moved between the lodges. Everything was quiet, but soon family and friends would return for the Winter Spirit Dances, and the village would be crowded again. She stood a moment longer, squinting into the morning light that flooded the long, broad valley, and then she started home.

A STARVING DOG

※ Chapter 8 ※

After the long, cold winter, Kaya and her family left the sheltered canyons of Salmon River Country and journeyed upland to dig fresh kouse roots—the delicious, nourishing food her people needed. This spring they'd come to the beautiful Palouse Prairie, where they'd meet Nimíipuu and other peoples with whom they shared these root fields. There would be many reunions with friends and much trading, dancing, games, and horse racing, too.

But Kaya's family had chosen to come here for another reason—they'd promised to help Two Hawks, the boy who had escaped with Kaya from enemies while in Buffalo Country. He needed to get back to his own people, the Salish. Salish often came to the Palouse Prairie to dig roots and trade. A trader might take Two Hawks to his home. Kaya looked around for Two Hawks. He was herding horses with some other boys. She thought he looked happy, but she knew he badly missed his family.

Her grandmother touched Kaya's arm. "Why are you watching the boys when you should be working?" Kautsa asked. Her usually gentle voice was stern. "And you're frowning. What have I taught you about making yourself ready to dig roots?"

"You've told me not to have bad thoughts that might make the roots hide themselves," Kaya said. "And I must stay away from sad thoughts, too, so the roots won't make us sick when we eat them."

"Aa-heh," Kautsa said. "You must have a pure heart to do your work well and be worthy of your namesake."

Kaya knew her grandmother was right, but she'd found that staying away from bad or sad thoughts was very, very difficult. Her younger sister, Speaking Rain, was still a captive of the enemies from Buffalo Country. Kaya's horse had been captured, too, and then traded away. And each time Kaya thought of Swan Circling's death, she had to fight to keep her heart from aching. Sometimes Kaya wished she could be a carefree child again, like her twin brothers, who were happily trying to sneak up on green racers and catch the little snakes with their bare hands.

"Will the root digging begin soon?" Kaya asked.

"Very soon!" Kautsa said with a smile. "Two women elders went to check the fields today. They brought good news. The roots are waiting for us. The roots are singing!"

Kaya felt a shiver down her back. Hun-ya-wat, the Creator, sent both animals and plants so that Nimíipuu might have food to live. But if anyone treated these gifts disrespectfully, then the fish, the deer, the berries, or the roots might not give themselves to The People. Kaya prayed that nothing she had said or done—or thought—would cause her people to go hungry.

Kautsa put her strong arm around Kaya's shoulder. "I see that something troubles you, Granddaughter." Now she spoke gently.

"I still have a lot of sadness in me," Kaya admitted. "Do you think I should keep away from the digging?"

"Only you know your own heart," Kautsa said.

"I want to work with you and the others!" Kaya blurted. "I want to do my part, like my namesake always did."

"Of course you do!" Kautsa said. She squeezed Kaya to her and then held her at arm's length to look at her. "But you've told me your heart is troubled. For now, let others work with the food until your dark thoughts leave you and the time of mourning is over in your heart. You can join us when your thoughts are clear again."

"Aa-heh," Kaya said with a sigh. She knew her grandmother's advice was wise, but the realization that she wouldn't be working with the other girls and women made her feel even lonelier.

Kautsa glanced at the sun, high overhead. "We need firewood so I can get our meal started," she said.

"I'll get some," Kaya said at once. She was glad to walk across the greening field to the stream, which was rushing with the runoff of melted snow. As she went, she saw horses rolling on their backs to shed their thick winter coats. When she bent to pick up driftwood, she saw the first early blooms of yellowbells. Soon her thoughts were lighter, but still she felt uneasy, as if she were being watched. Were the Stick People peeking at her? Was a bear prowling nearby, hungry after its long winter sleep? She stood and looked around.

Kaya let her gaze move slowly across the scrub, searching for any little sign of what might be hidden there. In a moment she saw the amber glint of two eyes watching her through the leaves. Those eyes reminded her of something—what? Then she remembered the yellow eyes of the wolf that had led her through the snowstorm toward her father when she was stranded on the Buffalo Trail. But a wolf wouldn't come so close to where people camped. She crouched. Now she made out a pale muzzle and a black nose, the head of a large dog.

Drawn by the dog's searching gaze, Kaya inched closer. The dog moved slowly out of the bushes toward her, the tip of its tail wagging slightly. She could see scars on its back and shoulders. She could also see its ribs showing plainly. It wasn't one of the camp dogs, which she knew well. Maybe it had come here with another band. But why had it strayed off alone?

"I don't have any food for you, but your people will feed you. Go back to them. Go!"

The dog gazed at Kaya for a long moment, perhaps hoping she'd change her mind. Then it slipped away into the bushes, quickly vanishing.

As soon as the dog disappeared, Kaya had the sinking feeling that she'd just done a terrible thing. She remembered that when she and her sister were slaves, fed only on scraps, she'd vowed never again to chase off the starving dogs that sometimes appeared at the camp. Kaya whistled to call the dog back to her side. But it was too late—the lone dog was gone.

NEWBORN PUPPIES

Chapter 9

THE NEXT MORNING KAYA WENT TO
the stream as the first rays of sun shone through the
blanket of mist hanging over the water. Sandpipers were
stepping along the shoreline, and a raccoon searched for
crawfish in the shallows. Kaya dipped in her water basket
and then drank from her cupped hand. It was a quiet
morning, though she could hear the voices of the boys
taking their morning swim downstream.

As Kaya drank, she saw Lone Dog appear on a rise a
short distance away and then look around warily as it trotted to the stream to drink. Kaya set down her water basket
and waited until Lone Dog had drunk its fill. "Tawts
may-we!" Kaya greeted the dog softly. "Look, here's food
for you." She held out the bone she'd brought with her on
the chance she would see the dog.

Lone Dog's ears pricked up and it stood with its head
lifted, sniffing all the scents traveling over the water and
land. Kaya knew Lone Dog smelled the bone, and Kaya
put down the bone by the stream. She picked up her basket

and started walking, as if she didn't have a thought for the dog. When she glanced over her shoulder, she saw Lone Dog seize the bone and lope off into the brush with it. In a moment the dog had disappeared.

Kaya looked for Lone Dog every time she went to the stream. She waited on the shore as long as she could, but Lone Dog didn't appear. With her sister in captivity, Kaya often felt alone—like the dog. After Kaya took the water basket she had filled to her tepee, she went out again looking for Lone Dog.

Not far from camp, Kaya heard the soft, muffled cries of some kind of baby animal. She followed the sounds until she came to a hollowed-out circle beneath a rocky overhang. When Kaya crouched, she made out Lone Dog's yellow eyes gazing over the top of the nest, her face barely visible through the long grass.

"Tawts may-we," Kaya said gently. She placed the food she'd brought at the edge of the nest. "Here, you must be hungry."

Lone Dog sniffed the meaty bone and then shifted and rose to her feet so she could eat. When she stood, Kaya saw four little newborn puppies tumble onto their sides. They looked to Kaya more like ground squirrels than dogs. Their eyes weren't open yet, but they found one another by the warmth of their bodies and crept close together to fall

Kaya placed the food she'd brought at the edge of the nest.
"Here, you must be hungry."

fast asleep. Gnawing the bone, Lone Dog lay down beside
them again. The pups started nursing, their paws pushing
at their mother's belly.

"Aa-heh, you know how to take care of your pups,"
Kaya murmured to her. "I'll come visit you again soon."

Every day now, more and more people arrived at the
digging fields of the Palouse Prairie. This was a very good
place for digging kouse. It was also a very good market for
traders. Every day Kaya kept a lookout for the arrival of
Salish traders—she hoped they'd take Two Hawks back to
his family.

One afternoon, Two Hawks spotted traders hauling
hide tepee covers that looked like those of his people.

"Get your horse," Toe-ta told Two Hawks. "Kaya, come
with me on my horse. Let's see if these men are Salish."
He put his hand on Two Hawks's shoulder. "If they are,
we'll trade this boy to them for a worn-out moccasin. That
would be an even trade, wouldn't it?"

Two Hawks grinned at Toe-ta's joke. Then his glance
caught Kaya's, and his smile dimmed. She saw that he was
very happy—and also a little sad. Of course, he wanted to
get back to his home again. But now he felt at home with
her people, too.

The traders were indeed Salish, and that night Kaya's

family celebrated the return of Two Hawks to his people. Eetsa prepared a hearty meal of deer meat, berries, and kouse mush.

Afterward, the men talked. Because Two Hawks now spoke both Nimíipuu and the Salish language, he acted as interpreter. Sometimes they used sign language, too. Toe-ta asked one of the traders if he had seen or heard of his little daughter, a blind girl?

The trader frowned sadly. *I have not heard of the girl you describe,* he signed.

Kaya clasped her hands tightly to keep from crying. But now Two Hawks turned to look her in the eye. "You helped me and brought me to my family," he said to her. "I give my word that I'll try to find your sister and bring her to you."

Kaya blinked back her unshed tears. Two Hawks was her friend after all. "Kat-see-yow-yow," she said to him gratefully.

Kaya found comfort with Lone Dog and her pups. She loved watching the pups grow and change. Now, as Kaya approached them, the puppies turned toward her voice. The largest pup, which she called *Tatlo* because he still made her think of a ground squirrel, peeked over the side of the nest.

"Are you glad to see me?" Kaya asked Lone Dog, who lay among her puppies. Lone Dog's tail wagged as Kaya patted her and then stroked Tatlo's soft little ears.

As Kaya stroked the three other pups, Lone Dog jumped out of the nest and took the bone Kaya had brought her. She carried it off a short way and lay down to chew on it. She was leaving her puppies more and more often, though she still stayed nearby to protect them. Soon Lone Dog would start to wean them, and then Kaya hoped to bring Lone Dog and her family home to join the tribe's dog pack.

A few weeks later, Kaya piled some deerskins onto a travois and hitched it to one of the tribe's pack horses. As Kaya rode out to the dog den on the hillside, she considered her plans. Lone Dog had weaned her pups, and Kaya knew they were at an age when they should get accustomed to other dogs and to people, too. She thought that if she took the pups to the village with her, maybe she could lure Lone Dog to follow. She hoped Lone Dog would live by their tepee and be her special dog now.

The pups were prancing about in front of the den. Tatlo had a small bone in his mouth, and the other three pups were chasing after him, trying to get it. Lone Dog lay on the hillside above her den with her head resting on her paws. When Kaya slid off her horse, Lone Dog got to her feet and stretched. Then she came to lean affectionately against Kaya's legs. Kaya scratched the dog's back just above her tail. "Your pups are growing fast, aren't they?" Kaya said to her friend. "Now they can become part of our dog pack."

Lone Dog looked toward her pups wrestling for the bone and then back at Kaya. Would this solitary dog allow her pups to live among people?

"And I hope you'll come to live with me, too," Kaya said softly.

Lone Dog looked away. After a moment, she went back to the hillside and lay down again. She seemed to be thinking over what Kaya had said.

Kaya rounded up the puppies and put them into the makeshift nest on the travois. They curled up together, as if pleased to be going on a ride. Kaya mounted the horse and called, "Come, Lone Dog! Come!" Hoping that Lone Dog would follow, she began to ride slowly toward the path that led to the village. When she glanced over her shoulder, Lone Dog was trotting down the hillside to follow them.

But Kaya's worries were far from over. Lone Dog didn't seem to be at ease around people or the other dogs. When Kaya was in the camp, Lone Dog stayed near her side. But when Kaya left the camp, Lone Dog ran off by herself into the hills, sometimes staying away all night.

The season for digging roots was coming to an end. Soon everyone would leave the Palouse Prairie and journey to the meadows to dig camas there. Kaya worried that Lone Dog might not follow her when they broke camp, although her pups had joined the dog pack.

On the morning the women began to pack up all their belongings for the journey to the camas meadows, Kaya went looking for Lone Dog. Kaya looked all around the camp, calling her name. Where was she? By the time the women had rolled up all the tule mats and stashed the tepee poles to be used the next year, Lone Dog was still missing. In her heart, Kaya knew that Lone Dog had gone on her way—alone—as she needed to be.

As Kaya was helping the twins climb onto a travois, she felt a tug at the hem of her dress. It was Tatlo, pulling at her skirt and begging to play.

When Kaya ignored him, he began to sniff the bundles piled up near the horses. She heard him give his puppy growl and then saw him drag something from one of the bundles. With another growl, he started shaking what he'd found—it was Speaking Rain's doll!

"Tatlo, that's not a toy for you!" Kaya

cried. "Bring that to me!" She knew if she chased him, he'd run away from her with the precious doll. So she sat on the ground to encourage him to come closer. Tatlo paused, his head cocked. Then he trotted to Kaya and dropped the doll into her lap, his whole body wiggling as if he knew he'd done something good.

"Tawts, Tatlo!" Kaya said. She pushed the doll behind her and lifted the pup onto her lap. "Are you telling me you're going to help me find my sister someday?" she asked him.

Tatlo put his paws on Kaya's shoulders and looked at her with his amber eyes. Then he nipped her braids and licked her cheek and her chin. Kaya couldn't help but laugh as the rough little tongue tickled her face.

"Jump down, now," Kaya told him. But instead of jumping down, Tatlo turned around and around until he'd curled up in her lap. As soon as he laid his head on Kaya's legs, he was asleep.

Kaya gently stroked the sleeping puppy. His muzzle was pale, like Lone Dog's, and his big paws meant he'd grow to be large, like her. "I think your mother sent you to be my dog now," Kaya whispered to him. "We have a long way to travel, and I'll be very glad to have you with me."

THE SOUND OF THE FALLS

※ Chapter 10 ※

LONG BEFORE KAYA COULD SEE
the waterfalls on the river ahead, she began to hear their
voices. She and her family were riding over hot, dry plains,
so the murmur of running water was a sweet promise. But
as they came closer to the river, that murmur grew into
a powerful song, like many men drumming. When the
riders crested the last hill and looked down at the shining
river, Kaya saw the falls plunging over black cliffs. Even
at this distance the falls roared like thunder. The earth
seemed to tremble.

Kaya's father, who rode ahead, signaled for everyone to
halt before beginning the steep descent from the bluffs into
the valley. He and other men and women dismounted and
began checking the heavy packs to make sure they were
tied tightly and wouldn't slip and injure a horse or rider.

Kaya dismounted and gazed down at the river valley.
Stony islands clustered in the river, white water sweeping
around them. Kaya saw large horse herds grazing on the
flatlands. Many fishing platforms of sticks lashed together

had been built out over the water. Hundreds of tepees and
lodges lined both shores as far upstream and downstream
as she could see. The villages were those of many different
peoples—some who lived on the river all year and others
who visited from the plains, the mountains, and the ocean
to fish and trade. Kaya's band, and many other bands
of Nimíipuu, were joining them for the yearly return of
salmon up the Big River.

Kaya shaded her eyes and peered at the mist that
rose like thick smoke from the waterfalls. She saw bright
rainbows arching low over the falls, and her heart lifted.
Rainbows were good signs. She hoped to meet up with her
friend Two Hawks here at the falls. He might have good
news of Kaya's sister Speaking Rain.

But Kaya knew that Two Hawks might bring bad news instead. He might have learned that Speaking Rain had been abandoned by their captors—or injured, or lost. For how could a blind girl get along without someone to care for her?

As if Tatlo sensed Kaya's troubled thoughts, the pup bounded up to her, his pink tongue hanging out. He was growing fast, and his legs were getting long. Kaya bent down and put her face against his soft ear. "You'll help me find my sister, won't you?" she whispered. He licked her hand, his tail wagging in circles, as if he were saying, *I'll try.*

When Kaya followed her mother and the other women to the riverbank the next morning, the men and boys were already fishing. Some spearfished from rocky outcroppings along the shore. Others stood on sturdy platforms built out over the falls. They held their long-handled dip nets down into the crashing waters. When a salmon leaped into a dip net, the force of the current closed the net around it. It took great strength to lift a large, struggling fish, and if a man was pulled into the rushing water, he could be swept over the falls and drowned. For safety, the men tied lines around their waists and secured the lines to rocks. Kaya shuddered as she saw Toe-ta and the others leaning over the raging waters.

The men's work was difficult and dangerous, but the women and girls worked hard, too. All day Kaya helped carry the heavy salmon the men caught to the women who cleaned the fish and sliced them into thin strips.

As Kaya walked with Kautsa to their village upstream above the falls, she looked back down the valley at the villages that crowded the shore. "I've been watching for Salish people to arrive," she said. "Two Hawks might come with them."

"They could be on the other side of the river," Kautsa said. "Two women came across today in a canoe to trade with us. I don't speak their language, but Crane Song knows it. The traders told her that newcomers from the north were putting up tepees over there. Their tepees were made of hide, like Two Hawks's people have."

Kaya felt a shiver of hope. "Couldn't I cross the river with the traders and see who the newcomers are? I could cross back later with some fishermen."

Kautsa looked kindly into Kaya's eyes. "The traders tied their canoe upstream. Surely they'll have room for you. Take them some finger cakes as a gift."

Kaya ran into her tepee and put a handful of kouse cakes into the bag she wore on her belt. Then she had an idea. She took Speaking Rain's doll from her pack and tucked it into her belt. If, somehow, she found her sister, she wanted to put the beloved doll into her arms—a sign that she'd never lost hope they'd be together again.

Tatlo was sleeping in the shade beside the tepee. When Kaya came out with the doll, he jumped up and licked her chin. Then he sniffed the doll and licked it, too.

"Do you want to come with me?" Kaya asked. Tatlo barked twice, as if saying *Aa-heh!* He ran ahead as she raced up the shore to where two women were putting bundles into a dugout cedar canoe.

Kaya asked in sign language, *May I cross the river with you?*

With her hands, the elder woman said, *Come with us.*

Gratefully, Kaya gave her the kouse cakes and climbed into the canoe. Tatlo jumped in right behind her.

The young woman knelt in the prow of the canoe, and the elder woman sat in the stern. The elder woman expertly guided the canoe away from shore. Soon they were paddling across a place where the water was shallower and quieter than the rest of the river. This was a prized fishing place because it was easy to see salmon in the clear, smoothly running water.

Kaya saw the boys Raven and Fox Tail fishing together

on a little island just downstream. They'd tied their safety lines around the same rock, and they were taking turns using a big dip net. As Kaya watched, Raven dragged up the net with a large salmon twisting in it.

The many fish leaping and splashing around the canoe excited Tatlo. He put his feet up on the side and barked at them. "Get down!" Kaya said. "Down!" She grabbed the big pup by the scruff of his neck and tried to make him sit. But Tatlo was too excited to sit. When a salmon jumped right next to the canoe, he lunged and snapped at it—and toppled out of the canoe into the river! The surging current caught him and swept him downstream.

"Help my dog!" Kaya cried. The wind whipped her braids across her face and tore away her words. She watched in horror as Tatlo struggled to swim in the churning river. His paws thrashed the water, and his amber eyes looked about wildly. Each time he came up for air, the current dragged him under again. Surely he'd be swept down to the falls and killed on the rocks below!

The elder woman turned the canoe downstream, and the young woman paddled hard and fast. But Kaya knew there was no way they could catch up to Tatlo. Already the current had carried him downstream almost to the island.

Then she saw Raven looking their way. He quickly thrust the dip net back into the river. Fox Tail leaned out

"Help my dog!" Kaya cried.

and peered down into the wild water. Then, with a sweep,
Raven raised the net with something in it. Fox Tail grabbed
the handle, too, and steadied the heavy weight against
his body as he helped lift the net. It took a long moment
for Kaya to realize that it was Tatlo they lifted out of the
swirling water!

The elder woman guided the canoe toward the island.
By the time they beached on the stones, the boys had Tatlo
out of the net and on his feet. The pup was coughing water
and shaking it from his coat. His legs were wobbly, but
he managed to wag his tail when Kaya scrambled from
the canoe and knelt by him, pressing her face against his
drenched head.

"The current carried him right to us!" Raven yelled
over the river noise.

Then Fox Tail leaned toward Kaya with a sly grin. He
put his mouth near her ear and shouted, "Magpies don't
know how to take care of dogs!"

That awful nickname again! *But he's right,* she thought.
*I didn't take care of Tatlo. I should have held him every moment.
It's my fault he fell in.* Instead of hanging her head, she
looked Fox Tail right in the eye and flapped her arms like
a magpie. They both started laughing.

"Katsee-yow-yow!" she shouted so the boys could hear
her thanks. With Tatlo shivering against her legs, Kaya

climbed back into the canoe so that they could continue on
to the opposite shore.

Kaya made her way through the villages crowded
along the shore. Tatlo stayed right beside her, and his nose
twitched at all the new scents around them. Kaya's ears
buzzed with all the different languages she heard. From
time to time she stopped where women were cooking
and signed, *Where are the newcomers camped?* Always they
pointed east, so she kept walking upstream. At last she saw
several hide-covered tepees in a small circle. Could these
be Two Hawks's people? She ran, with Tatlo loping at her
side.

A young woman was unloading deerskin bags from
a travois. Kaya threw her the words, *What tribe are you?*

The young woman cocked her head and studied Kaya
closely. She signed, *I am Salish. What tribe are you?*

Kaya swept her hand from her ear down across her
chin, the sign for Nimíipuu. *Is Two Hawks with you?* she
signed. *He wintered with our people.*

Two Hawks told us about you, the young woman signed.
Right now he's fishing with the men. She motioned for Kaya
to follow her. As Kaya and the Salish woman walked
among the tepees, Tatlo sniffed the air a moment and then
bounced away and began ranging back and forth between

the tepees. "Tatlo! Come!" Kaya called, wanting to keep him close to her. When he didn't come, she ran after him.

Horses grazed near the tepees. Tatlo ran between them, his tail wagging, and headed for some small pines. Kaya followed. She saw a baby in a tee-kas propped against one of the pines. Tatlo was sniffing the girl who sat tending the baby. The girl's back was to Kaya, who was so intent on catching her pup that she didn't realize until she was only a few steps away that the girl was Speaking Rain!

"Sister! My sister!" Kaya cried. She felt tears sting her eyes as she went to her knees in front of Speaking Rain and seized her hand. "You're alive!"

"Kaya?" Speaking Rain hesitantly touched Kaya's face and then threw her arms around her shoulders. "Aa-heh, I'm alive! How did you find me?"

"I didn't find you," Kaya said. "My dog did! Tatlo knows your scent from your doll." She took the doll from her belt and placed it in Speaking Rain's lap. "I mended it for you and kept it safe. I knew we'd be together again!"

Speaking Rain clutched her doll to her chest, her smile shining like sun on the water. "Katsee-yow-yow," she said softly. "I prayed for you every day."

"Many times I've thought how hard it must have been for you after I escaped," Kaya said. "I shouldn't have gone!"

"But I wanted you to go!" Speaking Rain insisted. She

held her doll tightly. "I couldn't have kept up with you. Two Hawks told us how difficult your journey was."

"Was the woman who kept us in her tepee angry when she discovered I was gone? Did she whip you for helping me get away?"

"She was angry, but she didn't whip me," Speaking Rain said. "Her people were all hurrying to pack up and break camp. They wanted to get back to their own country before snow stranded them."

"Somehow you got away from them, too," Kaya said. "Or did they abandon you?"

Speaking Rain put her hand on Kaya's arm. "I don't know what happened, Sister. I found my way to the river to drink and wash. When I came back, everyone was gone. Maybe in their rush they forgot about me. I was alone."

"My poor sister!" Kaya breathed. "What did you do?"

"I tried to stay calm," Speaking Rain said. "I needed a place to sleep, to hide. I crawled through the thicket near the river until I found grass trampled where deer had bedded down. Low branches sheltered the nest. I decided to stay there. Even if I could have found a trail, I'd never have been able to follow it."

"Did you have any food?" Kaya asked.

"They'd taken all the food," Speaking Rain said. "I tried to eat grass, but I couldn't keep it down. After a few sleeps,

I was so weak that I could scarcely walk. And the nights grew colder and colder."

As Kaya listened to her sister's story, her heart hurt in her chest. "You must have been frightened," she said softly.

"I knew I would die, so I tried to make my spirit strong," Speaking Rain said. "But I drifted in and out of swirling dreams—awake, asleep? I didn't know anymore. Then I heard steps in the grass, steady ones—not a deer browsing. Someone was walking nearby. I moaned. The steps came closer, and then I felt a touch on my cheek."

Kaya leaned closer to her sister. "Who found you?"

"A Salish woman named White Braids. She took me in and brewed *wapalwaapal* for my fever. Every day she carried me into a sweat lodge and bathed me. She fed me broth, and then mush. She treated me as if I were her own child, and slowly I got stronger. When digging season came, I was able to travel with her to the root fields. That's where Two Hawks and his family found me."

"Is she here at the falls?" Kaya asked.

"Yes!" Speaking Rain replied. "Come with me and you can meet her."

"I have much to thank her for," Kaya said.

SMOKE ON THE WIND

Chapter 11

AFTER THE SALMON RUNS WERE
over on the Big River, Kaya's band traveled to higher
country where it was cooler for the summer. They set up
camp on Weippe Prairie in the foothills of the mountains
to dig roots, pick berries, and hunt.

At the end of summer, Nimíipuu women and girls
worked hard to collect as much food as possible before cold
weather came. Kaya couldn't work with the others because
she was still in mourning for her namesake, Swan Circling,
and her sad feelings would spoil the roots and berries.
Instead, she helped in other ways. Today, she and Speaking
Rain were given the job of looking after their little brothers
and some other small children in the shade of the pines.
"Let's pretend we're setting up a camp," Kaya suggested,
and the children nodded happily.

First, Kaya made split-willow horses so that the little
boys could play roundup. Then she made a fire ring of
pebbles so that the little girls could pretend to cook with
their miniature woven baskets. After that she set up a

small tepee frame of willow branches and covered it with several old tule mats. The play tepee was big enough to hold several small children, and they crawled inside.

Kaya and Speaking Rain lay at the tepee entrance, playing with the little toy horses. They made Kaya think of her beloved horse, Steps High. Although Kaya's heart was happy to have Speaking Rain back with her family, she feared she might never see Steps High again. Toe-ta told her she should choose another good mount, but Kaya was certain she could never love another horse as much as she did Steps High.

Speaking Rain sat up suddenly and frowned. "The smell of smoke on the wind is growing stronger," she said.

"You've got a nose as keen as a bear's," Kaya teased.

It seemed that because Kaya's sister was blind, Speaking Rain's sense of smell was especially sharp.

Speaking Rain lifted her chin and sniffed again. "It smells like a grass fire," she said. "Is a new one burning?"

Kaya shaded her eyes and gazed across the prairie. To the west, the sun blazed above red clouds massed at the horizon. To the east, a thick haze hung low over the Bitterroot Mountains, which she had crossed with Two Hawks after they made a daring escape from their enemies. When she drew a deep breath, smoke stung her nose, too. She licked her lips and tasted ash on her tongue. In this hot, dry season, lightning started many fires in the fields and forests, but she didn't see any new plumes of smoke in the surrounding hills. "Fires always flare up toward sundown when the wind rises," she said. "Are you troubled, Little Sister?"

"Aa-heh, I am troubled," Speaking Rain admitted. "Fire is like a mountain lion—you don't know when it might attack."

"I'd be troubled, too, if our scouts didn't always warn us of dangers," Kaya said.

"But our scouts are on the lookout for many things besides fires these days," Speaking Rain reminded her.

Kaya knew her sister was right. The scouts always kept watch for anything that might endanger the people, but now they were scouting out game trails and salt licks, too, as the best season for elk hunting approached. When Kaya thought of the elk hunts, she felt a shiver of pride. Toe-ta was one of the most experienced hunters, and the men had asked him to serve as headman for the hunts. Toe-ta's wyakin, a wolf, had given him strong hunting power, and the hunters needed to kill many elk to feed everyone through the long, cold season to come.

Speaking Rain cocked her head. "I hear horses coming this way," she said.

Kaya heard hoofbeats, too, and rose to her feet. Soon she could see a line of men riding out of the woods on the far side of the prairie. They were followed by women and children on horseback, pack horses, and other women whose mounts pulled loaded travois. Their dogs trotted alongside the horses, wagging their tails as the camp dogs rushed out to meet them.

"It's the hunting party that went over the Buffalo Trail last year to hunt," Kaya said. "Come on, let's welcome them back!"

The children didn't need urging—they were already hurrying to meet the buffalo hunters and the women who'd gone along with them to run the camp and prepare the meat. Kaya grabbed Speaking Rain's hand and they ran to greet the hunting party, too.

After everyone had greeted the hunters and the dried meat and hides had been distributed, the young men took their horses to the stream. When the horses had drunk their fill, the men splashed them with the cool water and then let the horses dry themselves by rolling in the grass. Kaya and Speaking Rain eagerly joined their young uncles, who always brought news and stories. Tatlo, growing big and long-legged now, left the milling dog pack and pressed himself against Kaya's legs.

Jumps Back, a short, easygoing fellow with a big grin, tugged Kaya's braid to tease her. "We've been gone so long that you girls are almost grown-up!" Jumps Back said. "I bet the boys serenade you with their flutes!"

"Not me!" Speaking Rain said with a giggle.

"Not me!" Kaya echoed her sister.

"Do your cousins still call you that silly nickname, Magpie?" Jumps Back asked, nudging Kaya with his arm and laughing.

Kaya laughed, too. "Nobody calls me Magpie any-more—except once in a while," she said. Kaya rarely heard the nickname she'd gotten when she neglected the twins, and Whipwoman switched all the children for her offense. To change the subject, Kaya pointed to a young stallion getting to his feet, bits of grass stuck in his black mane and tail. "I haven't seen that bay before. He looks fast."

"Aa-heh, he is fast," Jumps Back said. "Four sleeps ago we came upon a few horses led by a rogue stallion. He drove off his herd before we could get close, but this young stallion hung back from the others. I chased him hard on my best horse to get a rope on him. He'd been driven off by the older horse, I think."

"I didn't know there was a herd of untamed horses in this area," Kaya said.

"Some seem tame," Jumps Back said. "We think they're Nimíipuu horses. We're going to try to find them again before the snows come."

Kaya's pulse sped. "Nimíipuu horses!" she exclaimed. "The ones stolen from us last year? Was my horse one of them? Steps High has a star on her forehead, remember?" Hearing the excitement in Kaya's voice, Tatlo gazed up at her, his tail thumping against her leg.

Jumps Back rubbed his forehead as he thought hard. "I'm not sure," he said. "There were a few spotted horses in the herd, but I didn't get a good look."

"I guess I'm hoping for too much," Kaya said with disappointment. "I last saw my horse in Salish country. She couldn't be back in these mountains."

"Don't be too sure about that," Jumps Back said kindly.

"A stolen horse can wander off if it isn't tied to another horse while it gets accustomed to the herd. Your horse could have strayed and headed back this way, maybe searching for you. If we can track down those horses again, we'll find out."

Kaya was almost afraid to hope—it would hurt so badly to have her hopes dashed. Instead, she asked Many Deer, another member of the hunting party, "Did you make any good trades in your travels?"

"We met up with some hunters from the north," Many Deer said. He was known as a good hunter but was even better known for his short temper. "They wanted to trade for our best horses, but we refused. Instead, we traded a pack horse for three buffalo calfskin robes and some rawhide rope. That was a good trade!" His broad face flushed as he boasted. "And I got something they say came from the east, maybe from men with pale, hairy faces. Look here!" He opened his pack and took out a red-and-white bead, holding it out for Kaya to examine.

"It's pretty," Kaya said hesitantly. She had never seen people with pale skin, and she was curious about them.

Kaya leaned forward to take a better look at the pretty bead. "Would you trade it to me for a basket of dried salmon eggs?" she asked Many Deer.

At that moment Tatlo thrust his muzzle into Many Deer's pack, seized a small bundle in his sharp teeth, and shook it. Many Deer aimed a kick at Tatlo and caught the dog in the chest, sending him tumbling. "Stay out!" he hissed.

"My dog!" Kaya cried.

But Tatlo wasn't hurt. He lunged to his feet and placed himself between Kaya and Many Deer, baring his teeth and growling, ready to protect her at any cost.

Many Deer stepped back and put away the bead. "Forget it! Magpies have a lot to learn about making a trade!" he said scornfully.

Kaya held Tatlo firmly by the scruff of his neck and tried to think what Swan Circling would have done in a situation like this one. "Aa heh, you're right. I'm sorry my dog got into your pack," Kaya said after a moment. "Don't let that spoil your homecoming."

Jumps Back tapped Many Deer on the shoulder. "Come on," he said to the bad-tempered fellow. "We're tired and hungry. The boys will look after our horses while we eat." As the two men walked away, Jumps Back glanced at Kaya with a look of approval that said she'd handled the tense moment well.

Kaya took a deep breath to settle herself. More and more lately she'd been thinking about Swan Circling, the young warrior woman who gave Kaya her name. Kaya

realized that her thoughts were now lighter when she remembered her hero. Perhaps sad feelings would no longer
spoil the food that Kaya gathered. She wanted to talk over
her thoughts with her grandmother.

Toward sundown, Kaya found Kautsa cutting tule reeds
in a marshy place at the edge of the prairie. She bent low
to cut off the tall reeds. "Here you are, Granddaughter,"
Kautsa greeted her. "Come bundle up these tules so we
can take them to the village to dry."

Kaya carried an armload of tules to a sandy spot and
wrapped cord around them. "Kautsa, I've been thinking
about my namesake," Kaya said, careful not to say the
name of the dead aloud. "I've mourned her death for many
moons, and I think my heart feels lighter now."

"Are you sure?" Kautsa asked.

"I'm sure," Kaya said.

Kautsa stood up, put her hand on Kaya's shoulder, and
looked into her eyes. "If the time of mourning has passed
in your heart, will you join us to pick berries?"

"Aa-heh," Kaya said firmly. "My namesake was always
a strong worker. I want to live up to her name."

"Tawts! Let's take these tules back to the village,"
Kautsa said. "We need to prepare our evening meal."
Though she carried a heavy load, Kautsa walked with

vigorous strides. When they reached their tepee, she slid the bundle of tules off her shoulders and placed it near the doorway. "Wait here a moment, Granddaughter," she said as she ducked inside.

Kaya put down her bundle, too. In a moment Kautsa appeared again. In her hand was the hat she'd woven last winter for Kaya. Kaya had planned to wear the new hat this past spring when she dug roots for her First Foods Feast, but because she was in mourning, she hadn't been able to dig with the other girls and women. Kautsa had kept the hat with her own things.

"Soon we'll start berry picking, and after that we'll go with the hunters on the elk hunt," Kautsa said. "You'll need much strength in the days ahead if you're to work as your namesake did to feed the people. Now it's time for you to wear this." She placed the hat firmly on Kaya's head.

"Katsee-yow-yow," Kaya said softly, touching the single feather that decorated the top. She was eager to join the others again. And when they went with the hunters farther into the mountains, she might find her horse again, too. She narrowed her eyes as the evening wind carried more ash from distant fires. "I'm ready, Kautsa," she said.

"Now it's time for you to wear this," Kautsa said.

FOUND

Chapter 12

THE DAYS WERE GROWING SHORTER

now. Kaya heard owls screeching at night and saw geese flying high—signs that the coming winter would be a hard one. But berries were especially thick and plump this year, and the women and girls were able to pick and store a great many.

As the berry season came to an end, the band split up. Many journeyed down to Salmon River Country to set up their winter village in the sheltered valley there. Kaya traveled with her family and the hunting party higher into the mountains for the elk hunts. The men rode ahead, leading the way. The women and children followed with travois and pack horses. Raven, Fox Tail, and other young boys brought up the rear, driving extra horses to carry back the meat.

As they ascended the trail, Kaya looked out across steep, rocky hillsides split by stony gulches. Whirring ladybugs swarmed around the horses. The mountainsides glowed with deep green heather and red-orange huckleberry bushes. All around, a blue haze of smoke rose from the valleys and tinted the sky gray with ash. Though cold weather was not far off, the days were dry with no sign of rain—it was still the season of fires. The scouts constantly scanned the mountains and skies for signs of danger.

As the women set up the hunting camp, Kaya helped raise the tepees and then took the twins to where Kautsa and Brown Deer were preparing a meal. The boys were hungry, so Brown Deer gave them some pine nuts to nibble on while the deer meat cooked.

"Speaking Rain was glad to go down to Salmon River Country," Brown Deer said to Kaya.

"Aa-heh," Kaya agreed. "The fires in these mountains trouble her."

"I'm not afraid of fire," Sparrow boasted. "It can't hurt me!"

"Speaking Rain knows better—fire *can* hurt you," Brown Deer corrected him. She placed heated stones into the water in the cooking basket, stirring them so that they wouldn't scorch the basket.

"You must always respect the power of fire, Grandson," Kautsa added sternly as she put deer meat into the boiling water. "Fire is a great gift, but it has its dangers, too."

Kaya listened closely to her grandmother's warning, and she thought of Speaking Rain's worry about fires. She vowed to keep a sharp watch for them as she searched the surrounding countryside for her horse.

On the day before the hunt, Toe-ta hobbled the lead mare with a rope attached to her forelegs so that she couldn't wander away—he wanted the horses close by so that they could be easily rounded up before first light. He invited the hunters into his tepee to talk over plans for the hunt. Then the men gathered in the sweat lodge to make themselves clean. They thanked Hun-ya-wat for all His gifts and prayed that they would be worthy of the animals they needed for food. Kaya could hear their prayer songs rising up to the Creator.

That night everyone slept only a short while. Kaya heard Toe-ta rise in the dark to join the other men. They took their bows and arrows and put on headdresses of animal hides to disguise their human scent. Kaya, Eetsa, and Brown Deer quickly dressed. They rode away from the camp long before sunrise while the elk were still out feeding or returning to their bedding place from the salt lick.

Everyone dismounted near the valley where scouts had discovered the elk herd. Raven and the boys looked after the horses while the others went forward on foot. Quickly and quietly, the hunters took up positions at the narrow end of the valley, downwind from the elk. At the wide end of the valley, the women and girls fanned out in a broad V to drive the elk ahead of them, toward the waiting hunters.

They took care not to
startle the elk as they
moved slowly forward. If
the elk started running, they'd
plunge right past the hidden men, who
wouldn't be able to get clear shots with their arrows.

Kaya concentrated on the rustle of the elk moving
through the plumed bear grass. She could make out the
tips of their antlers, the flash of tan rumps, and the flickers
of ear tips. Even in the faint light she could see their tracks
on the worn game trails. Birds flew up all around her,
and from time to time a woman added her whistle to the
birdcalls, making her position known to the others.

Kaya remembered that she should be on the lookout for
fires. She scanned the mountain slope at the far end of the
valley. There was no sign of smoke on the plateau there,
but shapes moved among the pines, and she thought she
heard a distant whinny. Holding her breath, she stood still
and peered through the dim light. Gradually she made out
horses emerging from the trees to graze. Kaya's heart sped.
Could that be the small herd that the buffalo hunters had
seen? Could Steps High be with them? Kaya stared hard,
but the horses were too far off for her to see them clearly.

Kaya walked slowly forward again, but her racing
thoughts tumbled ahead, one over the other. What if she

slipped away from the others to get a better look at the horses? Maybe she could run up to the ridge for a better view and be back before the slow-moving elk herd reached the hunters. Or could she get a mount and ride close enough to the horses to whistle for Steps High if she was with them? Maybe she could round up the horses by herself—think how proud of her everyone would be!

Then, right in front of her, a pair of magpies flew out of their dome-shaped nest in a thorny bush. Crying boldly, they swooped upward among the other birds. Like an upraised hand, the sight of the magpies halted Kaya's racing thoughts. No, she must not act in such a way that she could be called Magpie ever again! It would be irresponsible to go after the horses by herself. She must follow in Swan Circling's footsteps and do only what was best for her people. She must work with the others so that there would be food for all. Whistling to signal her place in the group, she drove the elk forward to the waiting hunters.

The hunters' arrows were swift and their aim was true. Many elk gave themselves to Nimíipuu that morning. The women and girls prepared the meat to be packed and taken back to the camp, where they would cook some of it and dry the rest.

After the work was finished, Kaya couldn't wait any longer to talk to her father about the horse herd she'd seen at sunup. She found Toe-ta lifting a heavy bundle of meat onto a travois. Quickly, she described the horses she'd seen. "Jumps Back thinks they're our horses, Toe-ta. Steps High might be with them," she added, trying to contain her excitement.

Toe-ta put his firm hand on Kaya's shoulder. "Daughter, there's not much chance that your horse could be with that herd."

"But there is some chance, isn't there?" Kaya insisted. "Steps High could have strayed and come back this way."

Toe-ta thought for a long moment. "That's possible. We'll go look for the herd," he said. "I'll ask Raven to come along—he's not needed here right now. Let's see what we can find."

Kaya mounted a chestnut horse and rode out of the valley behind Raven and Toe-ta. They followed a game trail that led up toward the plateau where she'd seen horses grazing. The sun was high, and heat waves shimmered over the stony hillside. She was sure she'd seen the horses near those pines ahead, but now there was no sign of them. Had the lead mare taken the herd where it was cooler?

The trail left by the horses curved around the mountain and angled down the northern side. Kaya's gaze swept across slopes dotted with stunted firs and hunchbacked pines, bent down by past winter snows. Deep gulches

jagged down the mountain in every direction. The herd
could be in any one of them. Would she and Toe-ta and
Raven be able to find the horses before they had to rejoin
the hunting party, now a long way away?

The trail descended more steeply, and after a time they
found themselves in a narrow gulch where a thick grove
of tall firs grew. Spears of sunlight shafted down through
the canopy of branches, and the shadowed air was a little
cooler here. A small stream snaked through the trees.
Toe-ta signaled Kaya and Raven to halt their horses and let
them drink.

Kaya slipped off the chestnut horse she rode and knelt
upstream from the horses, drinking from her cupped
hands. The spring water was clean and cold, and she was
very grateful for it. When she glanced up again, she realized that the patches of dappled light were moving. Slowly
and silently, as if in a dream, a few horses appeared in
the grove—and then a few more. Coming to the watering
place, they stepped around fallen logs. When the lead mare
spotted intruders, she halted in her tracks, and the other
horses came to a stop behind her.

Kaya rose slowly to her feet. Toe-ta and Raven stood,
too. Then Toe-ta pointed to a horse barely visible behind
the others—a horse whose black forehead was marked
with a white star.

"Steps High!" Kaya whispered, almost afraid to breathe. In the same moment that she recognized her beloved horse, a long-legged, spotted foal crowded against Steps High's side—her horse had a little one!

Toe-ta climbed onto his stallion, Runner. Raven jumped back onto his own horse, too. "Whistle for your horse, Daughter," Toe-ta said softly as he tossed Kaya his rope. "She'll recognize your whistle. Call her to you."

Kaya's heart thudded, and her lips were dry. She licked them and managed to make the shrill whistle with which she'd called Steps High so many times. Her horse's ears shot up. Kaya whistled again, and Steps High began to move toward her, the foal following closely. "Come on, girl," Kaya urged her horse.

She whistled a third time, and the horse came to her. Steps High shuddered and then pushed her head affectionately against Kaya's shoulder. Kaya slipped the rope around Steps High's sleek neck and tied it. She ran her palm down the muzzle, soft as doeskin, and stroked the powerful jaw. She gazed into Steps High's dark, glistening eyes and felt her own fill with tears. "You've chosen to be my horse again," she whispered. "Katsee-yow-yow, my beautiful one!" Kaya turned to Toe-ta. "After all this time, can you believe we've found her?" she said.

But Toe-ta was studying the sky and the puffy,

"You've chosen to be my horse again," Kaya whispered.
"Katsee-yow-yow, my beautiful one!"

misshapen clouds that rose on the updrafts. He seemed worried. He said, "Wait here. I want to get a look at the countryside from the crest of that hill."

Kaya turned back to her horse, hardly believing that the moment she had dreamed about for so long was really happening. The foal nuzzled Steps High's flank. "Raven, look at her foal!" Kaya cried. She smiled at the foal's short brush of a tail, long legs, and big eyes. "Isn't he handsome with all the black spots? Won't he be—"

The sound of running hoofbeats interrupted her excited words. Toe-ta reined in Runner, whose hooves plowed into the sand, and motioned for Kaya to mount the chestnut horse again. "There's a fire just over that ridge. The wind is spreading it this way. We have to get out of this gulch." He kept his voice low, but she heard the warning in his tone.

Kaya glanced at the ridgeline. She saw a plume of smoke, but it was thin and white—it didn't look threatening. Three or four small spot fires burned near the top of the ridge, but the grass there was thin and sparse and the blazes no larger than cooking fires. What had Toe-ta seen that alarmed him so?

"Stay with me and keep close," Toe-ta said. He urged Runner ahead on the narrow game trail that ran down the gulch. Kaya jumped back on the chestnut, clasped Steps High's rope tightly, and followed her father, with Raven coming right behind. When she looked back again only moments later, more fires burned from sparks blown onto the scrub. And now she could hear something hissing and growling in the distance—like a mountain lion, the fire was leaping after them!

TRAPPED BY FIRE!

⁂ Chapter 13 ⁂

THE TWISTED GULCH THEY RODE
down was narrow and steep. Kaya rode as fast and as close
to Toe-ta as she could, keeping Steps High right behind
her. The foal ran, too, with his head at his mother's flank.
Across the gulch, small fires flapped along the ridge where
two winds met, pushing the fire back and forth between
them. That side, the north one, was thickly wooded with
juniper and fir trees. Kaya knew fire would burn fiercely
in the dense trees. The south side, where they rode, was
covered with bunchgrass and a few scattered pines. Fire
would burn more lightly on this side, though in the baking
sun, the air itself felt like fire. Kaya's eyes stung, and her
throat burned with every breath.

In a gust of wind, the wavering fire across the gulch
dipped down into the pines. Swiftly, it grew and grew.
Kaya watched in alarm as burning pinecones began to
swirl through the air, starting spot fires farther down the
slope. The smoke blackened and boiled upward. Fire began
to growl like a bear as it spread both up and down the

slope. Could it keep pace with them as they galloped their
horses down the gulch toward the open end and safety
on the plain beyond? The frantic horses couldn't be held
back—their instinct was only to escape.

Fearfully, Kaya looked across the gulch again. Heat
waves heaved and buckled above the spreading fire. Fiery
pine needles flew up like sparks. Burning twigs snapped
and cracked. Juniper trees began exploding in the intense
heat. But the open end of the gulch wasn't far off now—
was it? Kaya coughed and her eyes teared in the bitter
smoke. It was almost too hot now to breathe, and fear was
another fire in her chest. It was all she could do to cling
to her horse as it bolted behind Toe-ta's along the narrow
mountain goat trail.

With a roar, the ground fire on the north slope suddenly exploded into the treetops. Kaya saw the topmost
branches become a crimson tent of flames. The trees
burned from the tops down, like torches. A high wind
gusted up from the burning trees, making the boiling fires
hotter still. Wind snapped off branches with a sound like
bones cracking. It lifted logs into the air. The fire swirl
spun down to the bottom of the gulch and burst across
to the south slope below them. With a stab of pure terror,
Kaya realized that now it burned ahead of them, too, and
blankets of black smoke covered their escape route. The

panicked horses doubled back, bumping into one another, rearing and snorting in terror.

Kaya fought to stay on her plunging horse. Steps High reared again and again—would she fall backward on the slipping stones? Would the foal be trampled? Terrified, Kaya thought, *Have I found my horse only to lose her to fire?*

Toe-ta scanned the steep gulch, looking for a possible escape route over the ridge above them, but rimrock created a barrier just below the top. Could they find a way through the barrier? Kaya saw there was no choice—they had to try.

"Stay with me!" Toe-ta shouted over the howling roar. "Don't fall back!" His face was black with smoke and fierce with determination. Did he see a way out of the fiery trap? He gestured for Kaya and Raven to follow as he turned Runner toward the steep slope above them and urged the stallion upward. Raven's horse clambered up behind, its powerful haunches knotted with effort. Kaya forced the chestnut to follow and yanked on Steps High's rope to bring her along. The foal sprang over the rocks like a deer. Could the horses climb faster than the fire? Racing for their lives, they struggled upward.

Ashes, like flakes of snow, swirled across Kaya's sight. Burning embers fell onto her head and shoulders, stinging her hands when she brushed them away. On the loose stones, the horses' hooves slipped backward with each lunge until they gained a broad shelf not far below the rimrock barrier. The wind suddenly split the smoke, and for a moment Kaya saw the barrier clearly. Was that slash a crevice, a way through? Could they reach it? Again Toe-ta signaled for them to follow. Raven urged his horse after Toe-ta as the curtain of smoke closed behind them.

Before Kaya could follow, Steps High began to rear, whipping her head frantically from side to side. Kaya looked back—the foal wasn't there! Was it lost in the smoke, caught by the rushing fire? Frantic to find her foal, Steps High thrashed her head, tearing the rawhide rope from Kaya's grip. "Stop!" Kaya screamed. "Don't go back!" But, searching for her foal, Steps High had already plunged down the slope and vanished into the smoke.

Kaya tried to rein in the chestnut and turn it back after Steps High, but the panicked horse resisted. Without thinking twice, Kaya slipped off the chestnut, which pushed on up the slope where Toe-ta and Raven had disappeared. Kaya whirled around. Smoke surrounded her on all sides. Through the smoke, the sun was blood red. She stood alone. Her eyes felt blistered by the heat, and she cupped her hands over them. *I must be strong!* she thought. *I must not give up!*

When Kaya opened her eyes, Steps High was lunging

out of the blackness, her foal again at her side. She'd reclaimed her young one! As Steps High came near, Kaya leaped to catch the rawhide rope still encircling her neck. With her horse pulling her, Kaya stumbled alongside as they started uphill again. But she knew that on foot she couldn't keep up with her horse. Steps High would have to let Kaya ride if they were both to escape the fire.

Kaya saw her one chance to mount—if her horse threw her off, there would be no second try. Using all her remaining strength, Kaya scrambled onto a boulder, clasped Steps High's mane with both hands, and dragged herself onto her horse's back. Steps High shuddered but accepted Kaya's weight—her horse hadn't forgotten! Kaya rejoiced to be one again with Steps High. But which way should they go? She had no idea. The blowing smoke created a vast black cave with no opening. She'd seen a crevice in the barrier, but where was it? Which way might offer escape? If they went the wrong way, the fire would seize them!

Kaya heard a shrill whistle—one high, wavering note that cut through the roar. Could it be green wood singing in the flames? The whistle came again, more urgently. *Here! Here!* the whistle sang. Toe-ta must be whistling to her, signaling the way. She looked toward the sound but could see nothing. A gust of wind knifed through the smoke, and again she spotted the crevice, with a trail leading toward it.

Kaya turned Steps High along the trail toward the opening. With the foal pressing after, they gained the base of the barrier. Now Kaya felt wind pouring through the opening. Steps High felt the wind, too, and nosed forward, though she balked at the narrow passage. "Go!" Kaya urged her horse. Steps High moved one step and then another. Kaya's knees scraped the rocky sides as they slipped through the opening with the foal following behind. On the far side Kaya saw the ridgeline right above them. She clasped Steps High tightly with her knees and pressed her face into the black mane. "A little farther—we're almost there!" she cried. A few more steps and they had reached the crest.

Still panicked, Steps High started to tear down the other side, stones showering out from under her hooves. Toe-ta was riding hard back up the hill, looking for Kaya just as Steps High had searched for her foal. He swerved Runner, grasped the rope around Steps High's neck, and brought her to a standstill before she could injure herself and Kaya. Steps High's chest heaved, and her coat was drenched with lather. The foal's legs shook with fatigue. Kaya slumped forward. Her breath rasped in her throat, and her lungs ached from the smoke.

Toe-ta threw his arm around her shoulders. "Rest a moment!" he said. "We're safe here."

Kaya gazed around. The fire didn't threaten them because an earlier one had already burned off the hillside. Ash-gray patches of sage still smoldered. Juniper stumps smoked. In some places fire had swept by so quickly that it had only singed the scrub. Farther down the stony hillside, Raven and his horse made their way to the narrow river below, where deer and elk stood chest-high in the water. Raven glanced back and raised his hand to Kaya—they'd made it to safety!

"You fell behind," Toe-ta said in his deep voice. "I thought I'd lost you."

"Steps High ran away from me to find her foal," Kaya gasped. "When I caught her again, I lost my way. But you whistled to me! I followed your whistle and found the opening. Katsee-yow-yow, Toe-ta." Her voice shook, and she felt tears running down her cheeks.

Toe-ta wiped away her tears with his palm. "I'm proud of your courage, Daughter," he said. "You saved yourself, and your horse, too. But what was that whistle you heard?"

"Your whistle," Kaya repeated.

Gazing into her eyes, Toe-ta slowly shook his head. "I was headed for the river when I saw the chestnut mare without a rider. Right away, I started back after you. But I didn't whistle to you. That must have been the Stick People. They showed you the way."

"The Stick People?" Kaya asked.

"Aa-heh," Toe-ta said. "I think they saw you needed help, and they gave it."

Kaya's head was spinning, but she remembered she must leave a gift for the Stick People. "What can I give them?" she asked Toe-ta.

"We'll leave them many gifts," Toe-ta said. "Now let's get to the river. The horses need water, and we do, too." Still clasping Steps High's rope, he began to lead Kaya and her horse down the burned hillside, puffs of ashes rising at their feet.

GIFTS

Chapter 14

As THE HUNTING PARTY RODE OUT
of the mountains to join the rest of the band in Salmon
River Country, the skies turned gray with heavy clouds.
Soon the first autumn rains began to fall. After the long,
dry season of fires, the rain was a blessing. Kaya pulled
her deerskin robe over her head, but she lifted her face to
the rain. It would soon turn to snow, but now it bathed
her cheeks and forehead with a soft, light touch. The rain
dripped from the branches she rode under, raising sweet
scents of pine and fir. Drops of it beaded in Steps High's
mane and on her foal's eyelashes. Kaya stroked her horse's
warm, wet neck and smiled to see the foal, which she'd
named Sparks Flying, splashing through the shallow
stream.

Now deer and elk were coming down to lower country
to forage. As she rode across the clearing, Kaya saw a bull
elk running through the scrub. He lifted his legs high
and tilted back his head so that his huge antlers could slip
through the branches as he raced like a scout bringing a

message. Kaya's heart swelled. She felt how strongly she loved her beautiful homeland and all the creatures that shared it with Nimíipuu.

When the hunting party reached the wintering place, Tatlo burst from the village dog pack and came running to meet Kaya. Bounding alongside Steps High, he barked repeatedly as if to say, *You're back, you're back!* When Kaya dismounted, he licked her cheek over and over again with his warm, rough tongue.

Kaya turned out Steps High and Sparks Flying with the other horses. Then, with Tatlo at her side, she ran to find Speaking Rain. She had so much to tell her sister.

Kaya found Speaking Rain in the snug winter lodge, twining cord from shredded hemp. Kaya knelt in front of her sister and placed her hands on Speaking Rain's arm. "Tawts may-we," Kaya breathed. "I'm here again!"

"Tawts may-we!" Speaking Rain gently touched Kaya's fingers. "Is that pine pitch I smell on your hands? Did you get hurt?"

"My hands and arms got burned by falling embers, but I treated the burns with medicine that my namesake taught me to make," Kaya said. "You were right to be troubled about fires!"

Speaking Rain drew in a sharp breath. "What happened?"

Sitting at her sister's side, Kaya told Speaking Rain how she'd found Steps High and described their escape from the fire. "When we got back to the hunting camp, everyone thought we were ghosts, because we were covered in black from the smoke. Before we left that country, Toe-ta and some other men rounded up the other Nimíipuu horses," Kaya finished.

"And now you're back safely!" Speaking Rain had been listening intently, as though she could feel, and hear, and even see everything Kaya described. "Whistles! Your horse came to you because she recognized your whistle. Then the Stick People saved your lives with a whistle."

"Aa-heh," Kaya agreed. "Come with me now! Don't you want to stroke Steps High again? I know you love her, too. And you have to meet her foal! They're the most wonderful horses ever!"

The days grew shorter and darker, until it was time once again to prepare for the new year celebration. Family and friends would arrive soon, and they would enjoy feasting, dancing, and sharing stories. Kaya and Kautsa brought bowls of salmon and roots to one of the winter lodges to cook for the feast. "Stay with me a while," Kautsa said. "We've been so busy lately that we haven't had time to talk."

As Kautsa knelt to light the fire, Kaya gazed at her grandmother's kind face. Her black hair was streaked with gray and her forehead and cheeks were deeply creased. Firelight glittered in her dark eyes as she regarded Kaya thoughtfully.

"Granddaughter, you've already faced many tests of bravery. Your next test will be one of patience, and of trusting the wisdom of your elders," Kautsa said.

Kaya frowned. "What do you mean, Kautsa?"

"I'm speaking of your vision quest, Granddaughter— the vigil you must keep at the sacred place on the mountain," Kautsa said. "If your spirit is clear and you're prepared—and if you can hold on and not run away—then your wyakin will come to you there. But before that happens you'll be hungry and thirsty and exhausted by fasting and praying day and night. Are you afraid?"

Kaya clasped her elbows and asked herself, *Am I afraid?* She had certainly been afraid when enemies captured her. She had been afraid when she escaped and found her way home. She'd been frightened to think she'd lost her sister and her horse. And she'd been terrified when she was chased by the forest fire. But what she felt now wasn't fear—it was determination. "I'm not afraid, Kautsa," she said in a firm voice. "I'm ready to meet whatever comes."

"Why, that's exactly what your namesake would have

said!" Kautsa exclaimed. "You're more like her than you may know. Soon, I believe, you'll use her name. It will be so good for her name to come alive again!"

Kaya felt warm with gratitude when she thought again of Swan Circling's gift. Kaya wanted so much to take the name of her hero, and now her grandmother felt that the time was almost here.

From across the village, criers began calling out, "Visitors are coming! Get ready to greet them!"

"Saddle up your horse and go meet our visitors," Kautsa said, rising to her feet. "I'll light these other fires and make the lodge warm for our feast. Go on now, be quick!"

Kaya ran to get the beautiful saddle she'd received at the giveaway after Swan Circling's burial and then hurried to the horse herd nearby. Tatlo bounded along with her, snapping at snowflakes and tossing up snow with his nose. Steps High was pawing through the ice for grass with the other horses. When she heard Kaya's whistle, Steps High trotted to Kaya's side, snorting white plumes of breath.

Kaya thought her horse seemed almost as excited as her frisky dog. Kaya pressed her cheek to Steps High's muzzle and stroked her horse's chest, feeling the strong, loyal heart beating there. In response, Steps High arched her neck and nudged Kaya's shoulder. As Kaya cinched the saddle tightly, Sparks Flying crowded against his mother with his head high and ears forward as though he were eager to welcome visitors, too.

Kaya swung up into the saddle and settled her feet in the stirrups. "Come on, girl," she said to her horse, and then she slapped her leg to signal Tatlo to stay at her side. Urging Steps High into a run, Kaya galloped out to meet the visitors on their horses appearing over the horizon.

GLOSSARY
of Nez Perce Words

PHONETIC/NEZ PERCE	PRONUNCIATION	MEANING
aa-heh/´éehe	AA-heh	yes, that's right
eetsa/iice	EET-sah	mother
Hun-ya-wat/ Hanyaw´áat	hun-yah-WAHT	the Creator
katsee-yow-yow/ qe´ci´yew´yew´	KAHT-see-yow-yow	thank you
kautsa/qáaca´c	KOUT-sah	grandmother from mother's side
Kaya´aton´my´	ky-YAAH-a-ton-my	she who arranges rocks
Nimíipuu	nee-MEE-poo	The People; known today as the Nez Perce
pi-lah-ka/piláqá	pee-LAH-kah	grandfather from mother's side
Salish/Sélix	SAY-leesh	friends of the Nez Perce who live near them

In the story, Nez Perce words are spelled so that English readers can pronounce them. Here, you can also see how the words are spelled and spoken by the Nez Perce people.

PHONETIC/NEZ PERCE	PRONUNCIATION	MEANING
tatlo	TAHT-lo	ground squirrel
tawts/ta´c	TAWTS	good
tawts may-we/ ta´c méeywi	TAWTS MAY-wee	good morning
tee-kas/tikée´s	tee-KAHS	baby board or cradleboard
toe-ta/toot´a	TOH-tah	father
Wallowa/ Wal´áwa	wah-LAU-wa	Wallowa Valley in present-day Oregon
wapalwaapal	WAH-pul-WAAH-pul	western yarrow, a plant that helps stop bleeding
wyakin/wéeyekin	WHY-ah-kin	guardian spirit

INSIDE KAYA'S WORLD

KAYA'S WORLD IN 1764 WAS NOT
very different from the world her ancestors had known for
thousands of years. How could Kaya have known that by
the time her own grandchildren were grown, her world,
and the world of her ancestors, would be changed
forever?

In the same way Kaya knew to be careful
when she smelled smoke on the wind, many Nez
Perce people had visions that warned them to
be careful of the people with pale faces who
were beginning to come to their homeland.

Kaya would have been an elder herself
when the Nez Perces saw their first white
people in the fall of 1805. That's when the
men of the Lewis and Clark Expedition
stumbled out of the Bitterroot Mountains
and into a Nez Perce camp. The explorers
were starving and freezing. The Nez Perce
befriended the travelers and helped them
resume their journey. In later years, white

*A Shoshone woman named Sacagawea helped
guide the Lewis and Clark Expedition.*

missionaries and settlers came to Nez Perce country and were treated kindly, too.

In the 1840s, white prospectors, or people searching for gold, began trickling through Nez Perce country on the Oregon Trail. Some were infected with smallpox, measles, or other diseases that killed thousands of Nez Perces. That trickle of white people became a flood in 1850, when gold was discovered in the Pacific Northwest.

Over the next thirty years, the U.S. government took away most of the Nez Perces' homeland so that white people could settle on it. The settlers cut down forests and let their pigs eat the camas that the Nez Perce people depended on for food.

Prospectors charged onto the Nez Perce reservation to find gold, and the government did nothing about it.

The government set aside a small tract of land in Idaho for all Nez Perce people to live on called the Nez Perce Reservation.

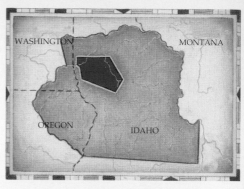

The U.S. government tried to force Indians on reservations to *assimilate*— to give up their traditional

An 1863 treaty reduced the reservation (brown area) to one-tenth its original size (red area), giving nearly 7 million acres to the U.S. government.

ways and live like white people. Children were placed in missionary schools to learn English and were punished if they spoke their own language. The reservation land was divided into small parcels and given to individual Indians to make a living by farming instead of hunting for and gathering everything they needed.

Some Nez Perce people adopted white ways. They gave up their buckskin clothing, cut their hair short, and became farmers.

The Nez Perce have lost much over the last 200 years, but they have never lost their spirit. History has scattered the people to different reservations and all over the world, breaking bonds that had been formed over generations. Yet, as the Nez Perce saying goes, "Wherever we go, we are always Nez Perce."

If Kaya lived among the Nez Perce people today, she'd be filled with renewed hope and pride. Much would surprise her. She'd meet computer engineers, scientists, students attending college, and children playing on basketball teams. She would also see children learning the Nez Perce language again, and storytellers passing along the same legends she would have told her own grandchildren. She'd see young girls learning traditional dances and parading their beautiful horses in honor of their ancestors, whose inspiring spirits live on to strengthen and nourish all Nez Perce people.

Kaya would know that the wisdom that she passed down to her grandchildren—the strength and spirit of Nimíipuu—would survive.

FIND MORE STORIES ABOUT THESE AMERICAN GIRL CHARACTERS AT BOOKSTORES AND AT AMERICANGIRL.COM:

a Nez Perce girl who loves daring adventures on horseback

a Jewish girl with a secret ambition to be an actress

who joins the war effort when Hawaii is attacked

whose big ideas get her into trouble—but also save the day

who finds the strength to lift her voice for those who can't

who fights for the right to play on the boys' basketball team